MW01137582

First published in 2017 by
Schism prɛss²

First edition
ISBN: 978-1537789118

Alternate portions of this work have previously appeared in
Unbroken Journal, and *Cartridge Lit.*

Printed in London, UK.

AMYGDALATROPOLIS

B. R. Yeager

Contents

Introduction

Being, Nothing, Same.

—Martin Heidegger

I – this nihility . . .

—Max Stirner

Absolute negativity is the authentic nature of selves and society.

—Tetsuro Watsuji

I love this phrase from an explorer—written while dying on the ice: "I don't regret this journey."

—Georges Bataille

[N]ihil videt et omnia videt.

—Angela of Foligno

What B. R. Yeager has given us in /1404er/, the protagonist of this book, is a grittily realistic, digital Dionysus who makes Mr. Robot look like Bo Peep. In overcoming all forms of external meaning—from morality to parental and state authority; sinking them down to their true abyss (*ihr wahres nichts*)[1]—what you hold in your hands, or in the soft light of your Computer's face is, accordingly, not a story, but a literally and literarily up-to-the-minute spiritual itinerary of one soul's journey into the heart of being—into the nothingness that lies coiled there like a worm.[2]

Worms creep. So does /1404er/. *He is a creep.* But then again, so was Christ: *Ego [...] sum vermis et non homo* (Psalm 22:6). Given the etymological origin of "hax0rz" in medieval arboriculture,[3] we should not be surprised to find a most apposite architectonic analogue for this masterful narrative of life lived through "real," hyper and virtual space-time in the great *summae* of the Middle Ages, and more specifically, then, in Bonaventure's *Itinerarium mentis in Deum*,[4] whose speculative theology, in accord with Western scholastic thought more generally, is comparable to the nave, tower and apse of a Gothic cathedral; "the clearest historical illustration of the system of architectural metaphor."[5] This ocular analog, which seems particularly apt in light of /1404er/'s vermicular movement through three modes of reality: mirroring the

---

[1] A more accurate translation here would read "their true nothing." In any case, this is Max Stirner quoted by Keiji Nishitani, *The Self-Overcoming of Nihilism* (Albany, NY: State University of New York Press, 1990), 120. Cf. "I – this nihility – shall drive out my various creations out of myself" (*Ibid.*).

[2] Cf. Jean-Paul Sartre, *Being and Nothingness: An Essay on Phenomenological Ontology*, trans. Hazel E. Barns (London and New York: Routledge, 2007), 45.

[3] See Kathleen E. Kennedy, *Medieval Hackers* (Brooklyn, NY: Punctum Books, 2015).

[4] See Bonaventure, *The Soul's Journey into God*, in *Bonaventure: The Soul's Journey into God; The Tree of Life; The Life of St. Francis*, trans. Ewert Cousins (Mahwah, NJ: Paulist Press, 1978), 51-116.

[5] Dennis Hollier, *Against Architecture: The Writings of Georges Bataille*, trans. Betsy Wing (Cambridge, MA: The MIT Press, 1998), 37.

movement of the cathedral's stone as it reaches up towards the heavens; reflecting the ascent through creation which Bonaventure describes in *The Soul's Journey*—culminating in "the skies above Hirasawa Pass, 9.04 PM his time. . . . A space perfect and vacuous"—would seem doubly apt given the fact that this "space with no thought or breath; no malevolence or consideration" arrives in the mode of light streaming through the cathedral's windows, which, for Bonaventure, reflected the downward movement of God expressing himself in his creation. "It was seven pictures. A figure laid in the grass. Small and pink, light clothes engulfed by hardening wet dark. A 8.5 x 11" white sheet resting next to her body, scratched with sharpie: 'sup fags ;) /1404er/06-17-2019 6. 30."

Undoubtedly a leading motif in *Amygdalatropolis*, light is everywhere; efflorescent: "LED light"; "the moon's reflected light"; "sun-less light beating through the drapery"; "the speed of light in vacuum, $c \sim= 3 \times 10^8$ m/s"; "light of the world turned to a smeared jelly filter"; "like frames of light captured from the past, and glossy empty bodies conjured by the Computer's face"; "eyes translating light from a stream"; from "streams and threads": "NDL"; "Clearnet"; "evil dark deep web"; "choice .onion sites": "gore"; "hurtcore"; "super hardcore snuff": "streams of men and women gone asunder beneath chainsaws and hunting knives"; "Yakuza finger mutilation"; "voluntary castration"; "kid getting raped to death". . . : "all the things he loved beneath the Computer's face." "A swollen blue oval atop half-dry porcelain white. Dime-sized eyes froze in odd directions, independent of each other. A thick viscous thread dangled out a black hole mouth, popped open forever. A scrap of paper reading *'sup /1404er/. 2-14-2026.*"

While true to the spirit of Bonaventure, who claimed, after Francis, that the soul (or mind, from Latin *mentis* via *mens*; encompassing the soul in its three faculties of memory, intelligence and will) could enter on this journey only "through the burning love of the Crucified,"[6] /1404er/'s mystical Christology comes closer to that of his contemporary, the Umbrian Franciscan tertiary Angela of Foligno, whose meditation on the fragmented body of Christ (on the bits and pieces of the lacerated body, so central to *Amygdalatropolis*) led to the dissolution of the subject:

> Once when I was meditating on the great suffering Christ endured on the cross, I was considering the nails, which, I had heard it said, had driven a little bit of the flesh of his hands and feet into the wood. And I desired to see at least that small amount of Christ's flesh which the nails had driven into the wood. And then such was my sorrow over the pain that Christ endured that I could no longer stand on my feet. I bent over and sat down; I stretched out my arms on the ground and inclined my head on them. Then Christ showed me his throat and arms.[7]

Angela's meditation on Christ's suffering attempts to fully explore the details of his torture so that this suffering comes alive for her and, in turn, for the reader of her *Book of Visions*. While meditation on the figure of a crucified Christ was widespread in the Middle Ages and, moreover, essential to the Christian mystic's identification with him, where Angela's practice diverges from this, construed more broadly, is in her contemplation of the bits and pieces of Christ's lacerated body, which gradually elides the gap between onlooker and object:

---

[6] Bonaventure, *The Soul's Journey,* 22.
[7] Angela of Foligno, *Complete Works*, trans. Paul Lachance (Mahwah, NJ: Paulist Press, 1993),145-46.

When I am in that darkness I do not remember anything about anything human, or the God-man, or anything which has a form. Nevertheless, I see all and I see nothing. As what I have spoken of withdraws and stays with me, I see the God-man. He draws my soul with great gentleness and he sometimes says to me; "You are I and I am you." I see, then, those eyes and that face so gracious and attractive as he leans to embrace me. In short, what proceeds from those eyes and that face is what I said that I saw in that previous darkness that comes from within, and that delights me so that I can say nothing of it. When I am in the God-man my soul is alive. And I am in the God-man much more than in the other vision of seeing God with darkness. The soul is alive in that vision concerning the God-man. The vision with darkness, however, draws me so much more that there is no comparison.[8]

Here, in her account of the twenty-sixth transformation of the soul, Angela describes the elision from the object-centered relationship that is desirous/loving to the encounter with and experience of the divine abyss of darkness or nothingness. This elision, which is masterfully recapitulated in *Amygdalatropolis*, was of central concern to the twentieth-century French philosopher Georges Bataille, a medievalist librarian by training, who claimed that it radically destabilizes the theological and soteriological assertions of traditional Christian mysticism.

Let us assume the reader is familiar with Bataille's oeuvre and skip to the part where, in focusing on passages of the *Book* in which Angela's soul seems to pass beyond the typical mystical experience of loving union with God into a darkness

---

[8] Angela, *Complete Works*, 205; translation modified.

or nothingness in which there is no semblance of satisfaction or completion,[9] he highlights a moment of absolute nihilism which corresponds beautifully to a brief gaming mise-en-scène in *Amygdalatropolis* that, getting right to the crux of the text, is punctuated by the refrain: "*Nothing you do will have any effect on the game.*" This refrain echoes Jean-Paul Sartre's critique of Bataille, which suggests that in his reading of mystical texts he reifies nothingness and makes of it a God and, moreover, that this absolute nihilism is an attempt—comparable to /1404er/'s—to escape temporality, history and responsibility through inner experience.[10]

---

[9] See *ibid.*, 202 and 204, respectively, and Georges Bataille, *Inner Experience*, trans. Leslie Anne Boldt (Albany, NY: State University of New York Press, 1988), 104.

[10] See Georges Bataille, *On Nietzsche*, trans. Stuart Kendall (Albany, NY: State University of New York Press, 2015), 173-80. For a great take on the entire debate between these two thinkers, see Peter Tracey Connor, *Georges Bataille and the Mysticism of Sin* (Baltimore: John Hopkins University Press, 2000), 119-27. In a cogent remark from Connor here, that really resonates with /1404er/, he says: "From Sartre's viewpoint, Bataille's quest for ecstasy is itself a form of project, and that, ipso facto, makes it into a value. And his values are less than clear: 'What's to prevent one from raping human beings, for you? I don't see why, according to your principles, one wouldn't rape human beings as one drinks a cup of coffee'" (123). An additional note to the reader, I've chosen to retain the French title of *On Nietzsche* throughout, as the prefix *Sur*, which in French can not only mean "on" but "over," better broaches the Nietzschean notion of *Surhomme* (superman or overman) and the Nishitanian notion of *Self-Overcoming* that this introduction is getting at. There is, accordingly, an *ethical* relation to the real—"rather than 'the ideal,' as per the superficial opinion of Western moralism" (Tim Themi, "Bataille and the Erotics of the Real," *Parrhesia*, 24 [2015]: 312-35; 312)—implicit in *Amygdalatropolis*, but supporting this claim here would require at least another thirty pages, so, I direct the reader instead to the aforementioned text in parentheses.

Inner experience is a loaded but crucial term for Bataille, and an important one for us here, both macroscopically—with respect to the overall trajectory of *Amygdalatropolis*—and microscopically—with respect to the trajectory of the boards therein, not least of all /1404er/, from which our protagonist takes his name:

> Thousands of boards, comprised of thread. Meccas poured down the Computer's face, and numbers of nameless becoming many and monument. Communion; devotion. To Japan and places mistaken for it, and the hobbies originating from there, and racial supremacy, and young children, the ruin of others, all rape and nothing. Everything imaginable. Cell bound into visibility, with digit guts and skin like pornography.

> ▶ **/1404er/ (Tue) 17:27:45 No.1000689696**
> dump the pics you shouldnt share

/1404er/ spent time at a few of the boards, but his favorite was /1404er/. The place he got his name from. Everyone was named /1404er/ there.

Visions of harm and waste of the weak. The color of pitch cut with red serif haunted house; the menu, gaudy rectangular light.

> **http://bas.ch.net/boards/1404er/**
> **/1404er/**
> *we do not argue with those who disagree with us*
> *we destroy them*

> **Active Users: 2986**

Catalogue

▶ **BOARD RULES (read 1st or be fukkked)**
▶ **dc body count 60 & rising**
▶ **this faggo stole my girl. destroy his life**
▶ **red rooms?**
▶ **just pasta or real**
▶ **flipping a coin to decide if i kill myself. first reply calls it.**
▶ **general Mussolini worship**
....

For Bataille, inner experience broaches a notion of community without authority, a community that simultaneously involves a dissolution of the subject and his or her sovereignty with and as the whole; where "[t]here a man is not distinguishable in any way from others: in him what is torrential is lost within others."[11] In Bataille's "Programme (Relative to *Acéphale*)," which, in 1936, publicized the program of a now notorious community that nevertheless remains to this day largely secret—but let us just say, as an aside, had things worked out, we'd no doubt be looking at a picture of a severed head. A 5 x 7" white sheet resting next to it, scratched with sharpie: 'sup fags ;) /1404er/20-01-1937 8. 30—he calls for a form of community "that is at once and unequivocally," to quote Jason Kemp Winfree, "a call for the destruction of community in any traditional sense. It is a call to do away with the bonds we

---

[11] This is undoubtedly Bataille speaking, and the quote extracted from *On Nietzsche*, but I can't for the life of me locate where at the time of writing. The general economic expenditure referred to and, moreover, the sense with which this is haunted by the thought that "[e]xistence cannot be at once autonomous and viable" (in *Ibid.*, 57) suggests to me it was gleaned from the section entitled "Part Two: Summit and Decline" (29-57).

most readily and thoughtlessly define as communal."[12] In *Sur Nietzche*, which was written almost a decade later, Bataille says, this community, which *a fortiori* involves communication, "cannot take place between one fully intact person and another," the community "wants beings who *question* being in themselves, who place their being at the limit of death, of nothingness."[13] Elsewhere, he says, this community, "without which, for us, nothing would exist, is assured by crime. 'Communication' is love, and love defiles those it unites."[14] And again, in more length:

> But these burning courses only replace the isolated being if that being consents, if not to annihilation, at least to *risk* itself, and in the same movement, *to risk* others.
>
> *All "communication" participates in suicide and crime.*
>
> Funereal horror accompanies it, disgust is its sign.
>
> And in this light evil appears—as a source of life!
>
> By destroying in myself, in others, the integrity of being, I open myself to communion, I attain a moral summit.
>
> And the summit is not *submission to*, it is *wanting* evil. It is the voluntary accord with sin, crime, evil. With an endless fate that demands that for some to live, others must die.[15]

---

[12] Jason Kemp Winfree, "The Contestation of Community," in *The Obsessions of Georges Bataille: Community and Communication*, eds., Andrew J. Mitchell and Jason Kemp Winfree (Albany, NY: State University of New York Press, 2009), 31-46; 33.

[13] Bataille, *On Nietzsche*, 33; original emphasis.

[14] *Ibid.*; emphasis removed from the original.

[15] *Ibid.*, 40; original emphasis.

▶ **/1404er/ (Thu) 19:46:01 No.10006856176**
>>>*10006856122*

Doesn't that apply to us? At least me and a lot of other people on here are much smarter and more powerful than the normalfags out. We're the return to the natural order. We draw power from the weak and ruin them to feed our strength. We bend reality to our whim. That could easily be called the same [. . .] So yeah, I guess that makes us society's elites.

▶ **/1404er/ (Thu) 19:48:59 No.10006856189**
>>>*10006856122*
>>>*10006856176*

your both faggots gtfo
"societys elites?" go back to grad school w that crap. som ppl just like seeing fuckedup shit. wtf is wrogn w u? fucing relax. life sucks. mite as well enjoy it #nolivesmatter

While an excursus on the nature of evil elaborated by Bataille is beyond the scope of the present text, it should suffice to say that in mirroring /1404er/s ". . . #nolivesmatter" response, it is precisely *beyond good and evil* in the Nietzschean sense, and as such is essentially innocent: "an authentic innocence, the absence of moral pretension and even, as a side effect, consciousness of evil [itself]."[16] In overcoming the notion of morality, and all related notions of external authority—including "God," the cultural construction, but also and especially apropos of Sartre, "history" and "temporality" (what communication wants, *in its essence*, Bataille says, is rejecting concern for the time to come)[17]—and insisting on the sovereignty of inner experience, much like our protagonist

---

[16] *Ibid.*, 49.
[17] See *Ibid.*, 41.

/1404er/, Bataille sought to differentiate the type of community it engenders from that sought by traditional strands of Christian mysticism, which, retaining a concern for salvation, project, and ends external to experience itself, he found slavish. In *Guilty*, for example, he states, "Angela of Foligno, in speaking of God, speaks in servitude."[18] And in *Inner Experience*, the first published volume of his *Atheological Summa*, which opens with a section entitled "Critique of Dogmatic Servitude (and of Mysticism)," he expresses the same ambivalence:

> By *inner experience* I understand that which one usually calls *mystical experience*: states of ecstasy, of rapture, at least of meditated emotion. But I am thinking less of *confessional* experience, to which one has had to adhere up to now, than of an experience laid bare, free of attachments, even of origin, of any confession whatsoever. This is why I don't like the word mystical.[19]

And yet, as Amy Hollywood has noted, "Bataille does not reject the term 'mystical' so much as appropriate it; he claims that inner experience better captures the mystic's experience than do their own dogmatic utterances."[20] This is brought to a barb in Part 4 of *Inner Experience,* where Bataille sketches an outline for a new mystical theology entitled "Post-Scriptum to the Torment/Torture [*supplice*] (or the New Mystical Theology)."

---

[18] Georges Bataille, *Guilty*, trans. Bruce Boone (San Francisco: Lapis Press, 1988), 16.

[19] Bataille, *Inner Experience*, 3; original emphasis.

[20] Amy Hollywood, *Sensible Ecstasy: Mysticism, Sexual Difference, and the Demands of History* (Chicago and London: The University of Chicago Press, 2002), 64.

Bataille commences this section by saying that, like Maurice Blanchot in *Thomas the Obscure*,[21] he wants a theology "which has only the unknown for its object." Such a theology would

> —have its principles and its end in the absence of salvation, in the renunciation of all hope,
> —affirm of inner experience that it is authority (but all authority expiates itself),
> —be contestation of itself and non-knowledge.[22]

This is followed by several chapters on God and conceptions of God central to Western philosophical and theological traditions. The God of the mystics is, he says, a God without aim or end, knowledge or salvation, and as such not a God at all in light of such Western conceptions. And yet, as before, we encounter ambivalence in the mystics' persistent return to such conceptions in spite of the textual shattering of them in their accounts of inner experience. Reflected in Bataille's writing, this ambivalence gives rise, on the one hand, to accounts of the mystics' God from the standpoint of darkness, dissolution, and nothingness, and on the other, from the standpoint of "the omniscient, omnipotent, and fully present source of unchanging transcendence and salvation." But Bataille plays on this ambivalence and, in a section entitled "God," subverts the latter conception on the basis of the former from the startling premise that God hates himself. Here, as Hollywood puts it succinctly, Bataille maintains that

> [o]nly when human beings are exhausted by existence and full of self-loathing do they turn to

[21] See Maurice Blanchot, *Thomas the Obscure*, trans. Robert Lamberton (New York: Station Hill Press, 1988).
[22] Bataille, *Inner Experience*, 102.

God as a source of salvation. Human self-hatred is reflected in the self-hatred of God. Bataille argues that "within human thought," God always conforms to humanity, which suggests that human conceptions of the divine are projections of human desire. God, as the projection of human desire, can never find rest and satisfaction because human desire is contradictory, as is apparent in mystical conceptions of the divine. Human beings desire fulfillment, and yet fulfillment of that desire would mark the end of desire itself. Following many of the mystics, Bataille posits human desire as ceaseless, endless, and only capable of momentary appeasement. For God (as desire) to know himself as God (as the fulfillment of all desire) would imply a satisfaction that God (as desire) cannot allow; thus God himself is, according to Bataille, an atheist.[23]

Though Hollywood doesn't draw attention to it, this trajectory is repeated in *Sur Nietzsche*, commencing with what is arguably the most important line in Bataille's oeuvre, and one I've yet to come across in her studies of sensible ecstasy:

> With the spite and obstinacy of a fly, I say insistently: *there is no wall between eroticism and mysticism!*
> It's ultimately comical; they use the same words, traffic in the same images, and ignore it!
> In the horror that she has of the stains of the body, grimacing with hatred, the mystic hypostatizes the fear that contracts her: she calls the positive object engendered by and perceived in this movement God. As is fitting, all the weight of this

---

[23] Hollywood, *Sensible Ecstasy*, 67.

operation rests on disgust. Located at a point of interference, on the one side there is the abyss (filth, the terrible perceived in the abyss with unable depths—time . . .) and on the other side, massive negation, closed off (like a paving stone, chastely, tragically closed off), from the abyss. *God!* We aren't finished with throwing human thought into this cry, this sickly appeal . . .

"If you were a mystic monk!"

"You would see God!"

An immutable being, which the movement about which I have spoken describes as definitive, a being that never was, never will be at risk.

I laugh at the kneeling unfortunates. They never stop saying, naively:

"Don't believe us! Look at us! We avoid consequences. We say God, but no! It's a person, a particular being. We speak to Him. We address Him by name: it's the God of Abraham, of Jacob. We put him on the same footing as another, *a personal being* . . ."

"A whore?"

". . . . ."

Human naiveté—the obtuse depths of the intelligence—permits all kinds of tragic mistakes, conspicuous trickeries. Like sewing a bull-dick on a bloodless saint, one doesn't hesitate to *risk it* . . . the immutable absolute! God lacerating the night of the universe with a scream (Jesus's *Eli Eli lama sabachtani*): is that not the summit of spite? God himself crying out, addressing God: "Why have you abandoned me?" Which is to say: "Why have I abandoned myself" Or more precisely: "What is

xiv

happening? Could I have forgotten myself to the point of *putting myself at risk?*"

In the night of the crucifixion, God, like bloody meat and like a woman's soiled spot, is the abyss whose negation he is.[24]

In drawing an equivalence between a piece of bloody meat and cum, Bataille is saying that sex and death are inviolably linked and, moreover, that this equivalence, which is already culturally given in *la petite mort* or "the little death" of orgasm, is the experience of God—and ergo equally transposable to the trajectory of *Inner Experience* being explored here qua atheism—"dying to oneself."[25] This is the longed-for swoon of /1404er/, "the same thirst for losing consciousness, the same after-taste of death"[26] we find in Bonaventure, who, as Jeffrey J. Kripal notes, further to Bataille in *Eroticism*, "was quite clear that the ecstasies of male mystics often produce real sexual fluids: '[I]n spiritualibus affectionibus carnals fluxus liquore maculantur,' he wrote [Within the spiritual affections, they are stained with the liquid of the carnal flow]."[27]

---

[24] Bataille, *On Nietzsche*, 133; original emphasis.

[25] Georges Bataille, *Eroticism*, trans. Mary Dalwood (London and New York: Penguin Books, 2012), 221-51; 232.

[26] Bataille, *Eroticism*, 241. Cf. "The longed-for swoon is thus the salient feature not only of man's sensuality but also of the experience of the mystics" (*Ibid.,* 240).

[27] Jeffrey J. Kripal, *Roads of Excess, Palaces of Wisdom: Eroticism and Reflexivity in the Study of Mysticism* (Chicago and London: University of Chicago Press, 2001), 72; italicization of Latin absent in the original. Cf. Bataille, *Eroticism*, 225 and 247, for original Latin and partial translation, respectively.

/1404er/ woke and touched his dick through his sweat pants. Small and soft but felt good in his hands.

The tank vid was alright but not too interesting. /1404er/ liked the way the head popped under the tread, and how the body flattened and split up the middle like a zipper. /1404er/ touched his dick, but only on top of his sweatpants. He didn't reach underneath, even after watching a fifth time. . . .

His dick was soft in his hands when he woke. . . .

He rubbed his dick, soft. It never got hard anymore. . . .

He ran his palms up, down and over his dick, both above and beneath his sweatpants. He twirled his dick through his fingers, flopping it against his thighs and the pants fabric. He couldn't make anything come out. . . .

His dick shrunk until it was almost absent. . . .

You advance on her and tap outward with your hatchet. Quick rhythmic lashings. The gap between your bodies close, and a gap emerges from between the woman's neck and shoulder. The gap stretches down to its belly. Red mist erupts past snapped collar bone. Its body spasms to the ground, grasping at its torso with cupped palms, to keep the insides from falling out. You flick your hatchet around and click the blunt end downward until the woman's face doesn't exist anymore. . . .

It looks real when you kill people. It was the only game /1404er/ ever wrote a user review for. Five stars and two short paragraphs. *It looks real when you kill people.* He wrote it twice. . . .

He spent hours of half-wake and strained, lengthy defecations just daydreaming the game's mechanics and design. Of vast brutality. The hues, shapes and numbers defining its spaces. A pocket of lawless promised land. A dream a Founding Father had. . . .

He admired it for opposing domestication. . . .

He touched his dick. He didn't cum but he almost felt happy. . . .

In an epigraph animating Hollywood's *Sensible Ecstasy,* Janet Kauffman asks "[w]here in the world can the body say I am in my element?" In a self-generated addendum it follows, "[t]he body strips to its flesh, and flame, and dives. When air gives out, and blues and greens simplify into dark, lips open the way lips open for kisses. But the body more fully desirous, recalcitrant in the extreme, says, even there. No, this is not the world I dreamed of. This is not the world."[28] In no small way inculcated in the virility that now largely escapes /1404er/, as it does the Bataille of *Sur Nietzsche,* "Part Two: Summit and Decline,"[29] this recalcitrance, a desensitized impotence—and, ultimately, estrangement—embodying a general ennui or boredom before the informational abyss, nevertheless broaches inner experience, which begins with dramatization and meditation on images, such as the above, "of explosion

---

[28] Hollywood, *Sensible Ecstasy,* vii.
[29] Bataille, *On Nietzsche*: "If I'm interested, *mystical states* are open to me. / Taking my distance from every faith, deprived of all hope, I have no motive to access these states" (55; original emphasis).

and of being lacerated—ripped to pieces,"[30] and reaches its asymptotic apogee in meditation on and thus before the void; a trajectory traced in *Inner Experience,* in the sections following "God" that are particularly indebted to Angela's *Book,* namely, "First Digression on Ecstasy before an Object" and "Second Digression on Ecstasy in the Void."

Here, having undermined traditional conceptions of the divine and appealed to the twenty-sixth or final transformation of Angela's soul, where she is immersed in God in nonlove and nothingness—

> Saint Angela of Foligno says: "One time my soul was elevated and I saw God in a clarity and fullness that I have never known to that point in such a full way. And I did not see any love there. I lost then that love that I bore in myself; I was made into nonlove. And then after that I saw him in a darkness, for he is a good so great that he cannot be thought or understood. And nothing of that which can be thought or understood approaches him" (*Livre de l'expérience* I, 105). And a little further on, ". . . The soul sees a nothingness and sees all things (*nihil videt et omnia videt*); my body is asleep; language is cut off. All the numerous and unspeakable signs of friendship God has given me, and all the words that he has spoken to me . . . are, I perceive, so below this good encountered in a darkness so great that I do not put my hope in them, that my hope may not rest in them" (id., 106).[31]

—Bataille seeks to similarly articulate the differential relation between ecstasy generated before an object and out of love or

---

[30] Bataille, *Guilty,* 32.
[31] Bataille, *Inner Experience,* 104.

desire for an other and that experienced in the void qua nonlove and nothingness. As Hollywood says, "Bataille's conception of the self-subverting nature of the divine suggests there will be no place for a positive object of meditation in his practice." But again, rather than simply rejecting the object-point of the mystics, he assimilates it, in his quest for inner experience, arguing that the object contemplated, the God-man or, in Angela's case, the bits and pieces of his lacerated body, "is not a divine object of emulation but a projection of the self, a dramatization of the self's dissolution":[32]

> I will say this, although it is obscure: the object in the experience is first a projection of a dramatic loss of self. It is the image of the subject. The subject attempts at first to go to one like itself. But having entered into inner experience, the subject is in quest of an object like itself, reduced to its interiority. In addition, the subject whose experience is in itself and from the beginning dramatic (it is loss of self) needs to objectify this dramatic character . . .
>
> But it is only a question there of a fellow human being. The point before me, reduced to the most paltry simplicity, is a person. At each instant of experience, this point can radiate arms, cry out, self itself ablaze.[33]

She dreams what most frightens her. She dreams a beast within her insides. So appalling a notion she will tip gas atop her head and light her self at the stake until the day she wakes. Over and over before she wakes, and she will not wake for decades.

---

[32] Hollywood, *Sensible Ecstasy*, 70.

[33] See *Ibid.,* 70, and Bataille, *Inner Experience*, 118.

She dreams in hypersleep, and one day she will wake. She will wake and all will be just as she left it.

No specter within or without her skin. Just immeasurable negative and two arms wrapped inflexible around a pair of flushed bodies who for decades would never move again.

In *Mysticism of Sin*, Peter Connor contends that Bataille had already begun to practice something like this meditative technique as early as 1922. In a letter to Marie-Louise Bataille, his cousin, written from Madrid circa this time, he describes a technique he uses to make himself "dream," which similarly involves staring at an object-point, in this case, an "absolutely inexpressive visage," until it induces a vision that "flows like the moon."[34] In *Inner Experience*, this inexpressive visage gives way to the alleged ecstatic face, "beautiful as a wasp," of a young man undergoing *lingchi* or "death by a thousand cuts":

> In any case, we can only project the object-point by drama. I had recourse to upsetting images. In particular, I would gaze at the photographic image—or sometimes the memory I have of it—of a Chinese man who must have been tortured in my lifetime. Of this torture, I had had in the past a series of successive representations. In the end, the patient writhed, his chest flayed, arms and legs cut off at the elbows and the knees. His hair standing on

---

[34] Connor, *Mysticism of Sin*, 167, n. 3.

end, hideous, haggard, striped with blood, beautiful as a wasp.[35]

The first in the series of representations of which Bataille speaks, of a man believed to have been executed on April 10, 1905, in the wake of the Boxer Rebellion, was given to him in 1925 by Dr. Adrien Borel, one of the first French psychoanalysts, and as suggested had a decisive role in his life

---

[35] Bataille, *Inner Experience*, 119. There is a possible missing causal link in the chain of events that led Bataille to meditate on the *lingchi* photographs suggested by Hollier in *Against Architecture*, and indeed by Bataille himself here, qua "upsetting images." Hollier recalls an incident in Madrid of 1922 where Bataille was present at a bullfight in which a famous torero, Granero, was killed by the bull. Of this incident, which he would later describe in *Story of the Eye* (trans. Jaochim Neugroschel [London and New York: Penguin Classics, 2001], 49-53), Bataille said: "Death's theatrical entrance in the midst of celebration, in the sunshine, seemed somehow obvious, expected, intolerable." In a brief excursus on "The Spectacle of Death" in Bataille's writing, Hollier links this incident through the Chinese men whose torture Bataille meditated on and the church of Saint Mary of the Conception in Rome, where in a chapel decorated with the bones of Capuchin monks buried there, death itself becomes material for a tomb, to the end of a lecture he gave on sin in 1945, where, following a tumultuous discussion, he described his position as follows: "I feel I have been put in a position toward you that is the opposite of someone placidly watching dismasted boats from the shore. I am certain the boat is dismasted. And I must insist on that. I have a great time and I look at the people on the shore, and laugh, I think, far harder than anyone looking at a dismasted boat from the shore can, because, in fact, in spite of everything, I cannot imagine anyone cruel enough to be able to see a dismasted boat from the shore and laugh with much abandon. But sinking is something else, one can have the time of one's life." Hollier concludes: "The spectator *touched* by what he *sees* (a knife blade, a bull's horn). Death appears, but it is in my gaze. I am part of what I see" (*Against Architecture*, 167-68; original emphasis).

and meditative practice—in *The Tears of Eros*, he says: "I have never stopped being obsessed by this image of pain at once ecstatic (?) and intolerable."[36] The question mark in parentheses is important, and we'll return to it in a footnote.[37] For now, let us just say, this ecstasy is related to the ecstasy brought on through Angela's imaginative recreation of Christ's passion, where, in moving from sensible identification with his suffering body to incorporation of that

---

[36] See Georges Bataille, *The Tears of Eros*, trans. Peter Connor (San Francisco: City Lights, 1989), 204-6; 206.

[37] As Hollywood notes in *Sensible Ecstasy*: "The claim is often made that Bataille insists on the victim's ecstasy . . . [But] [t]here is no evidence of this insistence in his wartime writings. The claim does appear in Bataille's last book, *Tears of Eros*, but it is attributed to Dumas and only reluctantly taken up by Bataille, despite his investment in the claim for the conjunction of anguish and ecstasy [see above] . . . He then goes on to ask what kind of 'voluptuous effect' this image would have had on the Marquis de Sade and insists on the close tie between ecstasy and eroticism, particularly sadism. But of course, the *victim* cannot be accused of sadism, suggesting that here Bataille critiques the sadism of his own meditative practice or dangerously elides the distinction between torturer and tortured" (303, n. 2; original emphasis). Hollywood goes further into this dangerous elision in her "Afterword" to Jeremy Biles and Kent L. Brintnall, eds., *Negative Ecstasies: Georges Bataille and the Study of Religion* (New York: Fordham University Press, 2015), 236-244, where, in a speculative tour-de-force (282-83, n. 8), she links the parenthetical question, through recent research into the missing publication dossier for *Tears of Eros*, to the French film *Martyrs* (2008; dir. Pascal Laugier); based on a cult of torturers obsessed by Bataille and the *lingchi* photographs. Cf. Timothy Brook, Jérôme Bourgon, and Gregory Blue, *Death by a Thousand Cuts* (Cambridge, MA: Harvard University Press, 2008), 222-42, and n. 35, above, which corresponds with Hollywood's fear here, that "there is some secret ecstasy lying on the edge of the body's destruction" (283).

body within her own ("You are I and I am you"), fragmentation, incorporation and simulation of the crucifixion leads to her joyful ecstasy:

> I just looked at two photographs of torture. These images have become familiar to me; one of them, nevertheless, is so horrible that it makes my heart skip a beat.

> I must have had to stop writing. I was, as I often am, sitting before an open window; I had just sat down when I fell into a sort of ecstasy. This time, I no longer doubted, as I did painfully the previous night, that such a state was more intense than erotic pleasure. I see nothing: *that* is neither visible or sensible. *That* makes me sad and heavy not to die. If I picture, in my anguish, all that I have loved, I must imagine furtive realities to which my love attached itself like so many clouds behind which *what* is *there* hid itself. *What* is *there* comes entirely from fright. Fright makes it happen: a violent fracas is required for *it to be there*.[38]

► out with the bathwater
► /1404er/ (Sat) 16:57:08 No.31004007619
Welp, our little one had a small mishap in the bath tonight.
Figured you guys would appreciate the pics.
It's cool. She wasn't shaping up to be that much fun anyway.
¯_(ツ)_/¯

Download: Bubye.jpg (2.5 mb)

---

[38] Bataille, *Guilty*, 32; original emphasis.

When an image of torture falls before my eyes, I can, in my fright, turn away. But I am, if I look at it, *outside myself* . . . The horrible sight of torture opens the sphere in which is disclosed (is delimited) my personal particularity, it opens it violently, it lacerates.[39]

▶/1404er/ (Sat) 17:41:55 No.31004007738
yr an inspiration to us all
Download: yay.jpg (2 MB)

/1404er/ clicked and another image emerged and swelled. A tiny face on a tangerine head. The tiny face held steady under a faucet head and torrent of furious clear liquid plunged deep down its mouth; down its throat and down its lungs. Puffing cheeks and squeezing eyes migraine-tight. /1404er/'s arms shook. His guts felt like they were about to rot out his orifices.

Bataille uses these two images—which, as Hollywood will go on to note, could, like the two images causally connecting *Amygdalatropolis* above, just as easily be "genuine 'snuff' photograph[s]"[40]—to attain inner experience; where his contemplation of the lacerated body of the tortured victim is analogous to Angela's contemplation of Christ's suffering, with one difference. Like Yeager, and by extension the images and texts that, throughout *Amygdalatropolis*, weave in and around the board /1404er/, Bataille refuses to succumb to a narrative that is salvific or compensatory. What is most important about the cross, he suggests, "is neither who is on it, nor the salvific nature of his suffering, but the suffering

---

[39] *Ibid.*, 35; original emphasis.
[40] Hollywood, *Sensible Ecstasy*, 90.

itself," which acts as the object-point through which the subject comes up against his or her own dissolution:

HENRY lays in darkness. The floors, walls and furniture cast blue and cinder, and some hum outside. His body shakes. He can't keep from crying and he's not quite sure why. Push him out of bed, and his room, and down the stairs into the kitchen and out the door.

Outside is a blurred unearthly dark. Purple mist hanging off the oxygen. Chunks of ground scooped from this dimension and swapped with negative space.

Push HENRY to the barn collapsed to rot and splinter. Push him WEST to the garden swollen with flies. Push him SOUTH to the chicken coops blown asunder among animal bone. Or push him back inside. Nothing you do will have any effect on the game.

Make him accept that there was nothing he could do to keep his loved ones safe forever. Make him accept that there was never any way to replace the bits of self that gradually fell away. Make him accept that he will come out of this world as nothing more than matter and electricity, and in time no one will know he was ever here to begin with. Press CTRL to close his eyes. Release to make him let go.

It was weird and short and kind of pointless, and mostly [/1404er/] didn't like the way it made his stomach feel. He shut off the Computer and pulled out its plug.

A bell chimes. HENRY's world twists into fractals and dancing golden hoops. Men and women without faces flicker as particles; their only lasting evidence. No thought or language. Slow dissolve. There is nothing else to do. There are no other endings.

In defamiliarizing the crucifixion, "whose cultural ubiquity has come to obscure the horror of the bodily [and more presciently, perhaps, embodied] torture it represents," Bataille, like Yeager, must use other images of woundedness and laceration in place of the Christ figure, if he is to assimilate the meditative and writing practices of medieval mysticism in his quest for inner experience. As Hollywood contends, the "object-point" becomes simply a "person," "a fellow human being":[41]

The young and seductive Chinese man of whom I spoke, left to the work of the executioner—I loved him with a love in which the sadistic instinct played no part: he communicated his pain to me or perhaps the excessive nature of his pain, and it was precisely that which I was seeking, not so as to take pleasure in it, but in order to ruin in me that which is opposed to ruin.[42]

NAME: HENRY KOWJOLSKI
AGE: 87
OCCUPATION: FARMER
HENRY HAS BEEN REAL FORGETFUL
LATELY, SO SOMETIMES HE NEEDS A

---

[41] *Ibid.*, 73.
[42] See *Ibid.*, and Bataille, *Inner Experience*, 120. Clearly, here, Bataille literally eschews the sadism of which he stands accused in the reading above (n. 37), coupled with Connor's in *Mysticism of Sin* (3-4), for instance.

*HELPING HAND WITH CHORES AROUND
THE FARM. HELP HIM KEEP THE PACE!*

Some of the most shocking aspects of *Amygdalatropolis*
mimic, in the contemporary world (or as Bataille would put it,
after the death of God *and* the end of history), the latter's
contemplation, in the modern world, of this man's suffering,
and Angela's contemplation, in the medieval world, of
Christ's crucifixion; moving, accordingly, from ecstasy or
anguish before the object to a greater ecstasy in the void,
whence "the soul sees a nothingness and sees all things (*nihil
videt et omnia videt*)." This move, which is Yeager's principle
semantic gesture, is articulated by Bataille in *Inner
Experience*:

> The movement prior to the ecstasy of non-
> knowledge is the ecstasy before an object (whether
> the latter be the pure point—as the renouncing of
> dogmatic beliefs would have—or some upsetting
> image). If this ecstasy before the object is at first
> given (as a "possible") and if I suppress afterwards
> the object—as contestation inevitably does—if for
> this reason I enter into anguish—into horror, into
> the night of non-knowledge—ecstasy is near and,
> when it sets in, sends me further into ruin than
> anything imaginable. If I had not known of the
> ecstasy before the object, I would not have reached
> ecstasy in the night. But *initiated* as I was in the
> object—and my initiation had represented the
> furthest penetration of the possible—I could, in
> night, only find a deeper ecstasy. From that moment
> night, non-knowledge, will each time be the path of
> ecstasy into which I will lose myself.[43]

---

[43] Bataille, *Inner Experience*, 123-24; original emphasis.

In this passage, Bataille articulates the relationship between his experience of unity with the suffering, lacerated, or tortured other qua object-point, upsetting image, and that with the divine abyss of darkness, nothingness, and unknowing. Yeager posits—or more accurately, discloses—a relationship between these two forms of experience in *Amygdalatropolis*, but unlike Bataille he does not completely elucidate the nature of the link between them; closer to Angela, perhaps, in simply suggesting a causal connection between /1404er/'s meditation and identification with Christ's passion qua object-point, "all the things he loved beneath his Computer's face," and his experience of the dissolution of the self and other—again, precisely the Computer's face; for Angela, the God-man: "When I am in that darkness I do not remember anything about anything human, or the God-man, or anything which has any form" / "/1404er/ didn't measure the hours, or days, or condition of his body. He didn't feel his hunger or fatigue. He was somewhere else now. Someplace separate from his walls, or room, or house, or the Computer and its history"—into a "space perfect and vacuous," at the end of the text. In this respect, the trajectory of our protagonist poignantly dovetails with that of Angela, whose reported last words were—"Oh unknown nothingness !" (o *nihil incognitum!*).[44]

Traditionally this statement has been taken to refer to the nothingness of Angela's created being, whereas Bataille suggests it may refer to the nothingness of the divine and, moreover, in his account of inner experience suggests the inextricability of the two.[45] But that Yeager explicitly interprets this nothingness as vacuity points beyond *Inner Experience* to the theopathic states of *Sur Nietzsche* where,

---

[44] Angela, *Complete Works*, 315-16.
[45] See Bataille, *Inner Experience*, 104, and Hollywood, *Sensible Ecstasy*, 69, respectively, for a sustained discussion of same.

eschewing the Orientalism of which he stands accused in *Sensible Ecstasy*,[46] Bataille has recourse to Zen Buddhism, and more specifically, *satori,* to explain them:

> In Zen, *satori* is intended only through comic subtleties. It is the pure immanence of a return to the self. In place of transcendence, ecstasy—in the most insane, the emptiest abyss—reveals an equality of the real with itself, of the absurd object with the absurd subject, of the time-object, which destroys by destroying itself, with the subject destroyed. This *equal* reality is situated in a sense further away than transcendence; it is, it seems to me, *the most distant possibility.*
>
> But I don't think that one can ever attain *satori* without first being shattered by suffering.
>
> It can only be attained without effort: the slightest thing provokes it from the outside, when it is not expected.
>
> The same passivity, absence of effort—and the erosion of pain—belongs to the *theopathic state*—in which divine transcendence is dissolved ["God alive in the clouds and internal bleeding," to quote Yeager]. In the *theopathic state,* the believer is himself God, the rapture in which he experiences equality of himself and God is a simple state and "without effect" ["He lay his palms flat on the desk, and stared into endless blue . . ."], however, like *satori*, situated *further away* than every conceivable rapture ["Beyond the blue an impenetrably cold vastness . . . encasing him in his world and all that had ever belonged to it"].[47]

---

[46] See Hollywood, *Sensible Ecstasy*, 88-91.

[47] Bataille, *On Nietzsche*, 141; original emphasis.

Bataille goes on to say he wasn't aware of the theopathic nature of the mystic's states when, in 1942, he attempted to elucidate their essence in *Inner Experience*. At that time, he writes, he himself had only attained states of laceration; "I only slipped into theopathy recently," he adds, remarking at once on the profound simplicity of this new state known to Zen, and in the final phase, Christian mysticism.[48] In drawing on Daisetsu Teitaro Suzuki's *Essays on Zen Buddhism*[49] in the previously unpublished notes accompanying this section, Bataille could be speaking explicitly of our protagonist /1404er/ when he says: "No graspable method permits one to attain *satori*, which assumes sudden derangement, the sudden opening of the spirit."[50] And a little further down in the section itself: "In [this] state of immanence—or *theopathy*—the fall into nothingness is not necessary. The mind itself is entirely penetrated by nothingness, is equal to nothingness."[51] For Bataille, who, as Stuart Kendall correctly contends, "writes with a hammer of descriptive insistence,"[52] this nothingness (*vide*) ought to be more precisely rendered as emptiness (*śūnyatā*)—*l'abîme le plus vide*, what he would call the emptiest abyss; that which, Yeager, in turn, terms perfect vacuity. In the Buddhist texts Bataille was reading while writing portions of *Sur Nietzsche*, reality is said to be empty. This emptiness, interpreted in Zen as "calm acceptance," becomes the Way wherein the Being Bataille posits as self-identical above, is simply the affirmation of self-sameness and

---

[48] *Ibid.*

[49] See D. T. Suzuki, *Essays on Zen Buddhism: First Series* (New York: Grove Press, 1961).

[50] Bataille, *On Nietzsche*, 268. Cf. "Inner Experience and Zen," *ibidem*, 171-72; 71.

[51] Bataille, *On Nietzsche*, 142; original emphasis.

[52] Stuart Kendall, "Translator's Introduction: The Wanderer and His Shadow," in *Ibid.,* xxi.

the negation of difference. This is the concluding point of *Amygdalatropolis*.

In starting out from the standpoint of relative nothingness, the Nietzschean experience of the self before the immanent abyss of the world, and ending up at the point of calm acceptance of the self-awareness of absolute nothingness, Yeager has cleverly, and with great literary economy, managed to elide the history of Western metaphysics—wherein a will-to-architecture or -structuration[53] has conditioned philosophical and theological thought at least since the time of Plato: wherein the "I AM" of the Hebrew bible is most presciently matched, perhaps, by the Husserlian "transcendental ego" or, if not, the "cogito" of Descartes, in any case, a construction of solid ground that wants to maintain itself, to assert its existence, even and especially when this manifests as the cultivation of a *desire* or *will* to nothingness—and map its spiritual journey onto /1404er/'s; a "journey," and he does refer to it specifically as such, that Keiji Nishitani would call "the self-overcoming of nihilism."[54] It is of absolutely no coincidence that /1404er/'s journey ends in Japan where *śūnyatā* forms the (foundationless) foundation of Eastern metaphysics and, to hark back to Bataille, a non-dualistic ontology of Being-Nothingness.[55] Put somewhat differently, the making present (*poiesis, ousia, techne*) of being/structure/self in *Amygdalatropolis* is knowingly—and as mentioned, masterfully so—the making of an excess, an excess which bears a very particular relation to nothingness, and more specifically, then, a self-understanding of the standpoint of absolute nothingness: "Japan is nothing," to

---

[53] See Kojin Karatani, *Architecture as Metaphor: Language, Number, Money* (Cambridge, MA: The MIT Press,1995).

[54] See the opening citation.

[55] For a good overview, see James W. Heisig, *Philosophers of Nothingness: An Essay on the Kyoto School* (Honolulu: University of Hawaii Press, 2001).

quote Yoshimi Takeuchi.[56] Or in the words of Otto Lehto, after Nishitani and my good friend Kojin Karatani:

> Japan is where East and West *meet*.
> Japan is where East and West go to *die*.
> . . . to be *revitalized* . . . and soon a new creature rises from the ashes of the old traditions, from this marriage of opposites: the "Buddha-Christ" (East-West). This child is a real accident without cause, an existence without substance. Beyond nihilism, we encounter true "*Being-as-Nothingness*."[57]

Crucially, for Nishitani, this requires approaching nihilism *nihilistically*, as Yeager does. There is absolutely no point, he says, "in 'studying' nihilism from the comfortable position of an armchair philosopher who wants to 'learn about the topic,'" as he puts it. "Insofar as the approach to nihilism is not itself nihilistic, I sense that it may abstract our understanding of the matter at hand"[58] . . . "if nihilism is anything," he adds, "it is first of all a problem of the self."[59] This is recapitulated somewhat differently by Bataille in the same section on *satori*, where he writes:

---

[56] Yoshimi Takeuchi quoted by H. G. Blocker and C. I. Starling, *Japanese Philosophy* (Albany, NY: State University of New York Press, 2001), 192.

[57] Otto Lehto, "Nothingness as Nihilism: Nishitani Keiji and Karatani Kojin," available from http://www.ottolehto.com/wp-content/uploads/2014/01/Otto-Lehto-Nothingness-as-Nihilism-Karatani-Kojin-and-Nishitani-Keiji-1.0.pdf (accessed 07/09/16); original emphasis.

[58] Lehto, "Nothingness as Nihilism," quoting Nishitani, *Self-Overcoming*, 1.

[59] Nishitani, *Self-Overcoming*, 1.

As strange as this may be, *pain is so rare* that we have recourse to art *so as not to miss it in the end.* We couldn't bear it if it struck us, if it took us completely by surprise, not being familiar with it. And we must certainly have knowledge of the nothingness that is revealed in it. The most common processes in life require that we lean out over the abyss. Not encountering the abyss in the suffering that comes to us, we have artificial abysses, that we provide for ourselves by reading, through shows, or, if we are talented, that we create.[60]

Yeager is this talent for us. His *straightforwardness with the worst*[61] opens before us the abyss of nothingness, which we, in turn, must open ourselves to, if we are to fully reap the rewards of this brilliant text, that attempts, like Bataille, and Angela before him, to engender in writing and in the reader the dissolution of subject and object that is inner experience. Through this dissolution communication occurs and a new community emerges—between Bataille, Angela and Yeager, and between Yeager and his projected readers, and more problematically, perhaps, between those readers and /1404er/.

Edia Connole

Dublin, Ireland
21 September, 2016.

---

[60] Bataille, *On Nietzsche*, 139-40; original emphasis.
[61] To borrow Bataille's turn-of-phrase in *Ibid.*, 140.

Thallus, you faggot, softer than rabbitfur,
or goosedown, or a sweet little earlobe,
or an old man's listless dick, lying in cobwebs and neglect.
And yet, when the full moon shows the other guests starting to nod and yawn,
you're grabbier than a plunging hurricane.
Give me back my housecoat, which you pounced on,
and my good Spanish flax table napkins, and the painted boxwood writing tablets,
which you keep on display, jerk, like they were heirlooms,
unstick them from your claws and give them back
or I'll use a whip to scribble some really embarrassing lines,
hot as the iron that brands disgrace on a common thief,
on your woolsoft sides and dainty little hands.
You'll get excited in a brand new way, your head will spin
like a boat caught out on the open sea when the winds go mad.

—Gaius Valerius Catullus, *"Carmen 25"*

The new countries offer a vast field for individual, violent activities which, in the metropolitan countries, would run up against certain prejudices, against a sober and orderly conception of life, and which, in the colonies, have greater freedom to develop and, consequently, to affirm their worth. Thus to a certain extent the colonies can serve as a safety valve for modern society. Even if this were their only value, it would be immense.

—Carl Siger, *Essai sur la colonisation*

AMYGDALATROPOLIS

I

We were never supposed to be here. Instead of flat plots chiseled and set adrift. The places where we gave in to things we couldn't otherwise imagine. An invisible plane, feeding off grass and grubs and refusal to bathe. Taking things that would never belong to us and building language from them. Worlds belonging to us and no other.

/1404er/ woke and touched his dick through his sweatpants. Small and soft but felt good in his hand. Always when he woke up, or was awake, and even in his sleep. Squeezed his eyes closed thirty minutes and sat swinging legs over bedside, standing and sitting again, but in the black gloss chair. He touched and shook (like an animal heart, or bleach-soaked bone) the BlueToothed pearlescent gloss chunk on his desk, and the Computer woke.

▶/1404er/ (Tue) 17:14:47 No.1000689679
Many meat eating animals consume pebbles and rocks to grind up meat for digestion. How come humans don't do this?

He always put the Computer to sleep before going to bed. Its boards would click and stir through the night behind its greyed-out face, like a yawn or stretch. He couldn't sleep with it turned off all the way. Now they were both awake.

►/1404er/ (Tue) 17:18:22 No.1000689684
Why does Keanu Reeves never seem to age?

He rubbed his eyes and his dick, squinting through the cartoon people and animals stretched across the Computer's face. 5:20 PM in the righthand corner.

►/1404er/ (Tue) 17:21:08 No.1000689689
how do u kill sum1 n there sleep

The Computer was a lot of things, but for /1404er/ the Computer was mostly the boards. The new town commons, stretched wide enough to fit the Earth's multitudes, though few thousands ever visited. The boards, by nature, could only mean so much to so many people.

And we and the century became pubescent and scratched out our names with fingernails until our features smeared blank and indiscernible. We printed our dicks out in plastic and chased women from their cities and homes. When our eyes peered their mouths we could process neither tooth nor tongue. Only negative space. A black hole. When we leered at their skin it was flesh of balloon.

Thousands of boards, comprised of thread. Meccas poured down the Computer's face, and numbers of nameless becoming many and monument. Communion; devotion. To Japan and places mistaken for it, and the hobbies originating from there, and racial supremacy, and young children, the ruin of others, all rape and nothing. Everything imaginable. Cell bound into visibility, with digit guts and skin like pornography.

►/1404er/ (Tue) 17:27:45 No.1000689696
dump the pics you shouldnt share

/1404er/ spent time at a few of the boards, but his favorite was /1404er/. The place he got his name from. Everyone was named /1404er/ there.

Visions of harm and waste of the weak. The color of pitch cut with red serif haunted house; the menu, gaudy rectangular light.

http://bas.ch.net/boards/1404er/
/1404er/

we do not argue with those who disagree with us
we destroy them

Active Users: 2986

Catalogue

►BOARD RULES (read 1st or be fukkked)
►dc body count 60 & rising
►this faggo stole my girl. destroy his life
►red rooms?
►just pasta or real
►flipping a coin to decide if i kill myself. first reply calls it.
►general Mussolini worship
....

Sometimes the boards sucked in the early evening. He refreshed every quarter minute, probing for fresh threads. He could've set it to refresh automatically, but he liked clicking the icon himself.

The room was four walls, a door, and slats of dead adolescent oak beneath ribs of dirty clothes. The room was shelves jutted from otherwise bare walls, toys placed atop. Mascots of some things he loved. The room was a mini-fridge and a microwave, and two small wastebaskets past the brim with empty instant kung-pao boxes. The room was a bed and a desk and a chair and the Computer, and /1404er/ staring in its face forever.

The boards' threads deformed and procreated with every second, and that night his board grew strange and beautiful. A thread—tiny bright thumbnail with words above—appeared. A rectangle cut with shrunken tan and blue blurs. Subject line just like something kind of magical. *afghani tank crushes guy.* Videos weren't usually as cool as quality raids, but almost always better than PA. Really, *really* great videos were sometimes better than anything /1404er/ had seen or felt. He clicked the rectangle.

Promised to fill them with knives and bullets and our very persons. Promised shit on front doorstops and suicide by officer. Promised it would never, ever end for them.

Islam always had some pretty cool stuff, but regular murder was better, like those kids killing idiots and old folks with hammers (years back, so it was sub-par definition, but through the buffers he could still see clear enough). Or that ice pick guy or the one with the pitbull.

/1404er/ liked some non-consensual, but only the real rough ones, and those were rare (the fakes didn't do anything for him, he told himself, but really he couldn't tell the difference half the time). He wasn't specifically into kids unless they got killed or hurt real bad, and those were the absolute hardest to come by. And even being safe, messing with kid stuff accelerated the likelihood of summoning The Vans exponentially.

It could be worth it. /1404er/ didn't really care about sex just by itself. At least watching it, or thinking about it much. A person's body felt disgusting.

►SWAT tutorial
►/1404er/ (Tue) 17:51:25 No.1000689711
So what's the process? I dont plan on doing it, im just genuinely curious.

►/1404er/ (Tue) 17:52:18 No.1000689719
I personally use burner phones to swat, like a cheap dollar store phone.

►/1404er/ (Tue) 17:55:36 No.1000689727
what he said. buy far from where you live, pay with cash, hide your face from cameras, etc etc

►/1404er/ (Tue) 17:59:04 No.1000689734
a lot of people drive to secluded payphones and do it from there.

I know you say you're just curious, but I really wouldn't get involved with swatting. It can be fucking funny, but if you actually end up killing someone you're nearly gaurenteed a visit from the party van.

►/1404er/ (Tue) 18:05:21 No.1000689749
Payphone would be the best option provided theres no security cameras around

2nd best is just to put as many loops in it as you possibly can. (1) Buy used prepaid phone from different state. (2) Use prepaid phone number to get a google number. (2) Make the call via public wifi. (3) Obviously through anything you're registering online you would use public wifi + NDL + 7 proxies

For added security only pick targets that reside in a different county than you

►/1404er/ (Tue) 18:10:02 No.1000689761
Using a burner phone or a payphone is fucking retarded. they all have IDs, serials, etc and payphones usually have cameras, and you also have to thinka bout DNA and other spooky stuff. they'll also get your general location, which is unacceptable.

i know using NOIP is the best way to go.
skype makes me uneasy. they collect a shitload of information about your computer.
google hangouts makes me uneasy since you have to use chrome and they use webrtc.

In the end, the only thing protecting you is an NDL and a caller id changer (if you use one), and thats privacy by policy, not by design.

The tank vid was alright but not too interesting. /1404er/ liked the way the head popped under the tread, and how the body flattened and split up the middle like a zipper. /1404er/ touched his dick, but only on top of his sweatpants. He didn't reach underneath, even after watching a fifth time.

▶/1404er/ (Tue) 18:12:45 No.1000689768
Let's also not forget they're recording all calls, including your voice. they can fingerprint your voice.

You'll need to use a TTS. But only if you don't want to get caught.

/1404er/ was born from video. His way into the threads. His eyes translating light from a stream. Before his eyes translated light from a stream he was only a person. Before the stream was a stream, it was a file. AVCHD, and prior to that just light reflected and refracted through systems of lenses. A copy of a living thing. Three living things and a fourth, all massed of matter and invisible crackle.

But /1404er/ was only around to witness the stream. The stream was a sequence of frames; LED light, flat and stuttered with buffer. Stuttered less than an eye can perceive. The stream reflected 30 frames and the puppy is in the boy's hands and a smile on his face and a smile on the face of the other boy, holding a bone of rectangle, eye-black and surrounded with pearl, and a smile on the face of the unseen transparent boy holding /1404er/'s eyes, allowing him entry into the world they stole. A chiseled bit of place atop terranean bridge blown out and sun-bleached and 30 frames and the boy has a smile on his face and the puppy is in his hands and his neck twisting back over his shoulder. And it's 30 frames and the boy's neck cranes back forward and there is the puppy leaving hands above all the world's emptiness.

And it's 30 frames and nothing holds the puppy and the railing is below her and all the world's emptiness and it's 30 frames and nothing holds the puppy and the railing is below and behind her and in a room there's a pistoning heart beneath a chest wrapped with fat strung arterial and it's 30 frames and nothing holds the puppy and the railing turns parallel with all

7

the crab-grassed sand and asphalt far below and beneath the royal nothing licked with sun and they're all snickering and it's 30 frames and the puppy is held by nothing and the railing is above her and so far and farther and farther. And it's like watching the Earth blot out the moon's reflected light and neanderthal ancestors scraping stone over meat. It's like dissolving into orgasm; belt-strapped windpipe and the immaculate weightless. A bris and a broken hymen.

The frames floated in the air, through the room. /1404er/ breathed in, letting them breach; letting them tumor through his lobes. Adding weight to his gravity. A layer of fat wrapped tight in his chest. A buffer.

He made the stream repeat, over and over, always breathing. Always letting it breach and fill his space, adding meat and corpulence to his form.

* * *

Language formed moat around our commonwealth. Words standing as close enough to nothing; scratches of symbol. Cavernous and quasi sub-masonic. Words not meant for ears, or paper or posterity. That was our strength and right to prosper. We kept separate the names. Names were refused. Names beget annihilation, like how hope ensures castration.

►fresh raid
►/1404er/ (Tue) 19:30:08 No.1000689820
femfags dogpiling this dudes employer cause "muh patriarchy," so lets send a message. I don't know all but the primes:

Beth Caven
Stephanie Mitchell
Mason Best
Carmen Reid

get addresses/emails/etc. and employers digits (lmao assuming they even work). be creative since cut and paste makes employers suspicious. and keep it realistic.

►/1404er/ (Tue) 19:34:52 No.1000689831
OP's a faggot but I'm game. you find her address yet? and does she have a twatter?

►**/1404er/ (Tue) 19:35:12 No.1000689834**
this her?
https://massgrab.onion.threads/Carmen-Colon
https://archive.is/qj872

►**/1404er/ (Tue) 19:36:28 No.1000689837**
scratch that already found the address/home
#
Current Address
1919 Gail Road
Ardentown, Delaware 19810
Home phone #
302 818 5921

Their blood didn't belong to us, nor the molted skins we grew of their crustings. Obscuring faces with poked eye holes. Spoken symbology, which through we watched our stirrings and forms. Crafting selves from stagnant amnio. Fingers grown holes and filled up with teeth. We couldn't believe. We could not believe.

►**/1404er/ (Tue) 19:38:36 No.1000689839**
>twatter
https://twitter.com/hereinmycar
^might be it

►**/1404er/ (Tue) 19:39:37 No.1000689841**
>>>*1000689839*
not it

The next post was a picture. A woman. Glasses between skin, above lime green cloth. An ugly smile etched wide.

▶/1404er/ (Tue) 19:49:31 No.1000689894
Meet Beth Caven. Cokewhore Ruth Bader, 29 y/o fembitch of Salt Lake City (I'm sure they just LOVE her). #'s 801-795-6363. YouTube is PolyWand

▶/1404er/ (Tue) 20:18:24 No.1000689937
What's her workplace? Are they open this late? If you DO contact her work, you should stick to the legitimate concerns about her harassing employers. Or whatever.

▶/1404er/ (Tue) 20:22:59 No.1000689941
lol the bitch (Beth) deleted all her videos. swatting? Or should we keep with this shitty letter writing campaign

▶/1404er/ (Tue) 20:39:10 No.1000689988
shes not picking up, but i left a funny message:
Download: bethmessage_32.avi (5.6 MB)

The thread grew for hours. Beth never picked up.

"Sweetie?" The inflection—a woman's—was Saccharin and upward through the particle wood in /1404er/'s door. "Are you up?"

"Yeah." /1404er/ swiveled in the chair toward the source of the voice, still invisible behind the door. "That's kind of a stupid question. What if I wasn't? Do *you* like getting woken up before you want to be?"

"I'm sorry, sweetie. Just curious." She inhaled deep and sharp. "Are we going to be able to spend some time with you today?"

"I'm working." And it was a sort of true. Beneath the threads and boards and interface, deep beneath the Computer's face, menageries of cracked diagnostic apps detected and cleared simple-but-to-layman IT fouls over at the Department of Mental Health. A legit basic-bitch white-hat gig. The money it provided afforded privacy, but not always without war. "What else?"

"It'd..." the voice behind the door slipped, almost cracking, but persevered. "...it'd just be great to see you today."

"Yup, great, but lots on my plate." /1404er/'s voice a sloppy blub of lisp. Unpracticed and raw. A lisp like a sopping shiv.

"Its been a long time since we've seen you and it'd...."

"Just real busy." He hacked and coughed, throat scraped up from inactivity.

"I have something for you."

Probably just a package he had ordered. /1404er/ ordered a lot of packages, and the voice always delivered them to his door. "Cool, thanks. Leave it. I'll check it out when I'm done." He coughed, and it exploded into belch. "Probably late."

"I'm sure they would be okay with you taking today off...."

"I. Am. Busy." Lisp filled with spit and piss. "*Busy*. I'm busy. Do you know even know what that means?" He waited for a word or whimper from behind the door, but nothing arrived. "It's cool though, because I actually *like* my job." Already blood on his tongue but there could be so much more. "Weird concept for you, I bet. If you hate your job, don't project on me." And the curb. "Don't blame me if you're not happy."

The voice from behind the door lost its capacity for language for the day. Tongue shrunken and vestigial. So the voice became the sound of unseen hands scuffing a package at the foot of the door. The voice became plodding soft slipper steps retreating down the hall.

He had already forgotten so much. It felt sharp across the ins of his skull. He couldn't remember where she worked, or even her profession.

Bodies and teeth emerged of whatever we gnawed. Our bodies and teeth were nothing before then. No calcium or discernible texture until we learned to devour others' skins, stretching them taught over our gums. The novel tactility. Our outgrowing of biology; splitting tongues and pissing over the last umbilical cords. The ends of grasslands and woods and laws of woman and man.

He fucked around on through the threads until he was sure the house was dead and slid across the hardwood on his socks. He slowly unlocked the door and pulled at the knob, fingers tensed white around. He edged his face over the doorway's lip and into the hall, rendered dark and stale like swarm and smoke.

He looked down at something circular and unfamiliar resting on the floor. A package, but not what was expected. A present. Brown and yellow and pink—light reflected and distorted through transparent carapace. He reached and pulled open its shell. A cake. A cake rimmed with soft-frost flowers. A cake ran through the top with a blue waxen staff and a red waxen whistle. Unlit candles, poured in the shape of a one and a six.

▶do you ever get excited when bad things happen?
▶**/1404er/ (Wed) 12:17:06 No.1000681387**
This morning I woke up and killed a box of cheerios when my buddy/roommate came down to the kitchen. he was the first one to tell me about the DC attacks yesterday so I figure'd I'd give him an update. I informed

him the death count was up to at least 117, to which he responded "Don't be so gleeful about it. It's creepy"

So guys: Is it creepy? I mean, yeah people are dying, but it's the wakeup call the world needs. And with politicians getting outspoken about our immigrant problems and with at least one saying "we need someone as strong as hitler" (the head of a right-wing party in france said that a few weeks ago, and a chick at that), made the nytimes actually say there's possibility for real change and push back against invaders.

And I mean come on. Its just people.

►/1404er/ (Wed) 12:19:37 No.1000681392
You're not wrong OP. Just don't show your abyss side to the normies

Almost four years before, the voice left her job and became a stay-at-home mother.

►/1404er/ (Wed) 01:22:19 No.1000681401
Yes, normies take it as creepy.
You have to be careful about being too honest with them. If you're lucky, though, you might find a friend or two IRL who you can be really honest with.

►/1404er/ (Wed) 01:23:45 No.1000681403
just explain why you are happy about the attack as intelligently as you did here and there'll be no problem

The facades' appeal was the dedication it implied. The need to commit to things. Not the we underneath, but the molt pulled over our figures. Feeding lies to fire like oxygen.

▶/1404er/ (Wed) 01:35:59 No.1000681425
does ebola worship fall into that category?

▶/1404er/ (Wed) 01:37:06 No.1000681429
I'm pretty fucking sure wishing for the death of billions of people counts. That being said: I LOVE YOU, EBOLA!

▶/1404er/ (Wed) 01:37:17 No.1000681430
always room for Ebola Worship :^)

▶/1404er/ (Wed) 01:43:12 No.1000681445
i know how you feel OP but you've got to keep a mask on it. to people who don't get, you sound like an edgy tryhard faggot. try to focus more on sounding concerned about the muslim invasion

▶/1404er/ (Wed) 01:44:01 No.1000681447
I LOVE YOU EBOLA!

▶/1404er/ (Wed) 02:01:13 No.1000681519
I remember when i was about 10 I saw some 3 year old fall out of the shopping cart he was sitting in and he hit his head on the floor and i remember in the second before he started crying and his mom began consoling him (they were at a dollar store, why didn't his mom just buy him some discount band aids lol. fuck that kid I hope he's a heroin addict now) I felt a rush of excitement at the

prospect that he might have been really very badly hurt, forever. I spent the next 25 years reflecting on that feeling.

▶/1404er/ (Wed) 02:06:31 No.1000681530
I LOVE YOU EBOLA!

* * *

III

No one knew who created it or other details of origin. Only that every character but the player had the name of a woman who was alive or had been at some point.

The year before, barely a week after /1404er/'s early graduation from homeschool, was one of a handful of times /1404er/'s parents actually worked it up to go ahead and drop the hammer. They said it was either get a job or go to Big Boy School, and they were so proud of the rare, inspired gumption they'd managed to conjure in themselves—so foreign to them and their offspring alike, it caught /1404er/ off balance. He folded almost instantly.

►Quick Reference (for evil!)
►/1404er/ (Wed) 04:41:53
No.1000681871
some tools you'll like
Wall Jumpah: put in some IPs and let it do the work for you
https://mega.co.nz/#!vqCbNQ0M! Z_xLfu0f_oi9IsXanUv_LGX3O0I RvtPac1w5jtCQP

List Parser

https://mega.co.nz/#!u30mJb5Q!
diiKuPPTQwNCmSpLvjEkhpalaO
z_1BlGAg

Clay's TampDown script:
http://pastebin.com/uR9t3Hqv

Or strip down to URLs only with
this other TampDown script:
http://pastebin.com/3Ac7Yt33

►**Can you drive stick?**
►**/1404er/ (Wed) 04:42:01**
No.1000681872
So can you?

►**/1404er/ (Wed) 04:43:59**
No.1000681875
Of course. I'm a fuckin badass

Dad worked in network security, and he spun his son's
education accordingly. /1404er/ actually took to the trade,
enjoying its simplest puzzles on a base, fundamental level. He
liked that it was work where he didn't need to be nice to
people, because he didn't really need to talk to them at all, and
he liked that he didn't have to lift boxes over his head or do
other things people do at regular-asshole jobs. All he needed
was the Computer's face spitting algorithms and minimal
concentration.

It paid well, too, so long as /1404er/ lived at home.

►**/1404er/ (Wed) 04:47:18**
No.1000681882
Crucifier:
http://pastebin.com/Ua8kjn99

If you want do do some TRI shit, you might want to start with this code. Updated to download CLST files but it will not parse out credentials.

Netcam Firmware:
http://pastebin.com/LzBQvx898

TP-Link Firmware:
http://pastebin.com/Eu0Q78Gy3

Eventually he earned enough to buy his parents out of the house's master bedroom. His father felt great pride when /1404er/ made the offer; so much so he talked mom into going along with it. He wanted his son to know that hard work could still pay off like it was supposed to.

►/1404er/ (Wed) 04:47:59 No.1000681883
Are there really people that can't? Do they just drive go-carts their whole lives?

►/1404er/ (Wed) 04:51:30 No.1000681899
6.5% of all vehicles sold in the USA for the first quarter of 2012 were manual transmission.
>that suggests 93.5% can't drive stick

Your body's a man naked draped in red riblets. Your mouth is a mouth plugged with rotten box teeth. The woods heave along with your breathing. Your fists wrap white around hot bricks.

The master bedroom was massive; almost double his old room. The floor became a bin for his dirty clothes (all his clothes were dirty, always). He didn't care about the extra space. All he wanted was a bathroom to himself.

►/1404er/ (Wed) 04:51:24
No.1000681898
Bemis LPX-9500
Retrieve admin password with backdoor. Backdoor can be modified for root access. Refer to "Network Exploits for the Average Bastard" by Ivan Grier for in-depth usage.

Dominion IP Extractor v2.0 by ZeramPr3th
http://pastebin.com/fdJ3he S39

PeepingTom v4.0 by ???
http://pastebin.com/35lucd a4aoe974kbcvx4fdf029x3p 3iqlk8e3d2

http://pastebin.com/Ty7sl9 0Hwy adds a "Foscam (and Knockoffs)" button to the PeepingTom "Add Camera" dropdown. You enter the camera IP, username, and password, and it automatically sets up the camera for you.

**►/1404er/ (Wed) 04:53:42
No.1000681902**
>>>that suggests 93.5% can't drive stick
SMH. It implies 93.5% of NEW car owners DON'T drive stick. My parents can both drive stick, but they haven't actually owned a manual tranny in years. My old roommate can drive stick but hasn't owned one since the '80s. Etc. BTW, I drive stick.

**►/1404er/ (Wed) 04:55:14
No.1000681910**
why are there so many americans that can only drive automatic then?

**►/1404er/ (Wed) 04:56:00
No.1000681911**
what fucking retard can't drive stick? fucking laughable

He got into the Department of Mental Health because of his aunt. He couldn't remember her name, but he knew she ran DMH's HR department. She arm-twisted her supes into creating a telecommuting position—a birthday present for her nephew, and a favor to her brother. (The family was very sympathetic to what they unanimously determined was /1404er/'s severe, as-of-yet undiagnosed agoraphobia.)

The world-sounds are bent guitar strings like beehives. Pulse of rubber valves. The woman has names stuck atop her head. Naked and face morphed screeching. Breasts swinging in pendulum, an improvisational design and system, manumit from hard physical. Amanda Watson. Or Stephanie Perry. Or Kelsey Winslow, above her head.

►/1404er/ (Wed) 04:58:22
No.1000681919
I'm British. Like everyone else over here I learned to drive a manual transmission but I choose to drive an automatic. It's like a having a servant change gear for you.

►/1404er/ (Wed) 04:59:29
No.1000681921
Eurofag here. I can drive stick but I really don't understand why so many people hate automatic. My parents own an automatic, and I see it as one of the most useful features in a car. So, why all the hate ?

►/1404er/ (Wed) 05:03:57
No.1000681930
most of my current cars are stick, during a time i didnt own an automatic i spent several months recovering from 2nd degree burns on my legs and a broken big toe on my driving foot and i still drove to and from work every day, also unboosted brakes. also my legs recovered mightier than

before but i still try not to put full
body weight on that toe.

**►/1404er/ (Wed) 05:01:28
No.1000681926**
what up faggots. This is great,
but i was wondering what do you
guys use for metadata
extraction/reading on
photos/video? i'm needing a GPS
location on some dumb bitchs
photos

*Break the body with a brick til it collapses. Break it with a
brick til it rants gibberish and floods. The bodies stop moving
but never disappear. Just pile and pile until turned into
ground. Pile higher than the trees. Pile high into mountains.*

He maintained a quarter of the networks and occasionally took
help desk tickets but mostly the algorithms beneath the
Computer's face handled the math. A thousand dollars
appeared in his checking account every two weeks.

**►/1404er/ (Wed) 05:07:42
No.1000681952**
try DumpTrust:
http://pastebin.com/oW7zp8Qyzx
just drag and drop and it spits out
any meta data (doesnt always
show up in the right place
though, but you should probably
be able to pick out the gps
coordinates)

**►/1404er/ (Wed) 05:06:44
No.1000681950**
people who only know to drive automatic have little sense about how to accelerate properly, i swear to god some of those dipshits think the accelerator should be pumped, they are just going up and down on the pedal pumping their car painfully slow up to cruising speed.

**►/1404er/ (Wed) 05:10:42
No.1000681969**
ah cool, this is perfect. just what i needed.

**►/1404er/ (Wed) 05:14:18
No.1000681988**
post pics when you get her

The rest of life was Japanese toon girls killed for wicked deeds. A movie about drug cartels. Batman comics.

80,690 North American animal slaughterers had jobs in 2014. All activities erode toward monotony.

**►/1404er/ (Wed) 05:11:39
No.1000681976**
yes. in my country only stupid bitches dont learn stick.

Eventually an article got forwarded around, saying how the women's names were siphoned from an Illinois maternity ward database. Trojans feeding names to the game. They eventually blocked access, and the women in the Computer's face lost their names. He stopped playing after that.

* * *

IV

Just mouths puckered like cracked anuses; castle turrets sunken through a planet of mud. Caribou drowned in piss. Gull wings run-through with fish hooks and broken skin on every surface.

6:06 AM in the Computer's face and /1404er/ fell asleep, guts clenched hot with thick chocolate turned caustic fluids. Pain of any degree would inebriate his capacities, and that morning he didn't even set the Computer to rest before rolling into bed (within a quarter hour it would drift into stasis, anyway). He just clutched at his belly and squeezed his eyes closed tight.

He didn't always dream when he slept. When he did, the dreams could almost be better than videos. Spaces full up with impossible spires and angles, and beautiful violent polygons. Dreams like strange and perfect games, stretched to take on galaxies and hells. Sprawls for him to kill in and fuck, like the men and grown-ups who inhabited spaces beyond his room. And sometimes his dreams weren't conjured from the blood in his brain or cock, but his miles of intestine, the frosting churned to ulcers like long thin knives.

Mother's face stretches taught across marble and mouth twisted upward and down and dark apricot nipples scraping foreskins like a hangnail, and belly folds around a dick reached far up to crack the atmosphere. Red, mustard and royal on perforated black and orb, within and outside matter.

The gods aren't good and she's warm deep between her, and he's just the specter of a dying race nuzzled hard to her lap.

►Dark Net Markets
►/1404er/ (Wed) 16:17:27 No.1000683174
put your links/reviews/qs/whatever here

►/1404er/ (Wed) 16:21:05 No.1000683182
Ordered 100x Red Supremes from YungCaligula. He takes one day to ship after order. Not a big problem cuz it arrived in a few days. Stealth was good, but I had about 5-10 pills that were broken or chipped. Not really a big deal because the regulars will take them. Excellent vendor going to try his MDMA next

https://YC888nggodsnotgud.onion

His dick was soft in his hand when he woke. The insides of his sweatpants glazed and crusted a warm white. Eyes kept squeezed tight. Gathering fragments of the body from his dream. His mother's body. Her expanded folds roped loose around his dick. White strung and collapsing through the galaxies. He tried to remember how she looked the last time he actually saw her face, and tried to remember how long it'd been. Images emerged from within the black beneath his eyelids, substantial and refocused. He remembered his mother's breasts, that time they were massive and unholy strapped under bra and button-down. He remembered the night spent imagining the feeling of riding her as she slept. Riding her til she noticed. Hours and hours eaten away, just picturing what it would be like.

►/1404er/ (Wed) 16:23:44 No.1000683188
Hey, I need help finding a one particular drug
that's illegal in my country. Not to get high.
Its for an abortion

He remembered the stash of Rohypnol he got off Blossoms
House (http://187jq7Bl_Ho88.onion) not long before The
Vans found it and shut it down. He'd only ordered it for shits
and giggles, nothing actually really serious. Just curiosity. And
he felt sexy hiding them in his desk.

►Personal Army requests
►/1404er/ (Wed) 17:11:58 No.1000683237
doing this so newfags can stop tracking
cancer through the rest of the board. have at
it

►/1404er/ (Wed) 18:02:35 No.1000683242
Name: Zvonimir Zepina
Gender: N/A
Country: Croatia
Age 15

Emo faggot framed me and my friends at
school for nothing and then acted like a
fucking victim afterwards. This guy is a
complete and utter fucktard.
Provokes and plays victim afterwards. Plus
his name is stupid.

Facebook:
https://www.facebook.com/zvonimir.zepina1
Phone number: 38599401951

He rubbed his dick, soft. It never got hard anymore. Spent and hung up constructing ways to get the capsules down his mother's throat. Maybe he wouldn't need the Rohypnol at all. He knew that lots of moms were into stuff with their kids. He'd seen it in streams and threads, and chatted with some of them, and they'd show him parts of their bodies, and he'd show them his, and they'd whisper about feeling each other's skin if only they could share the same space but alas. Years back. Before touching bodies made him nauseous. Before his mind learned to engorge the bodies with germs and excrement.

His mother—how she remained in his dreams and memory—broke through the sick. /1404er/ touched his dick and imagined her crying from him.

►/1404er/ (Wed) 18:09:27 No.1000683243
Jeanie Pelosi
32 Abram Street, Allston MA
857 318 4175

Ask Jeanie how many dead kids she has.
(It's three)

Ask her when she's going to get clean, and if she's ever going to get custody again.

Ask her, when she's going to try to kill herself again, if she'll do it in front of her remaining two kids.
Nothing personal

He could ask her. He could let her know it was okay. He could find a way to force the capsules down her throat, in such a way that everything could go back to normal the next day until forever.

►/1404er/ (Wed) 18:11:09 No.1000683238
This guy just sucks

Name:... Ken Belson
Address: 9 Palm Street, East Millinocket, ME 04430
Phone:.. 2077469419 (may be outdated)
DOB:.... January 11, 1975

[Contact]
Email:........ blueboy7458@gmail.com
Skype:........ blueboy7458
Last known IP: 72.83.67.81

[Social media acounts]
http://twitter.com/blueboy7458
http://youtube.com/blueboy7458
http://instagram.com/blueboy7458
http://www.reddit.com/r/blueboy7458

[Gaming accounts]
Battle.net Battletag: blueboy#7458
Diablo II: blueboy7458
League of Legends: blueboy7458
PLAYSTATION: blueboy
STEAM: blueboy7458
[STEAM_0:0:87301852]
(http://steamcommunity.com/profiles/873135
83174257310)
Imgur: blueboy7458

That should be enough.
Fuck him up.

With her, it wouldn't even feel like sex, or rape, if it had to be that way. New communion, like all the things he loved beneath the Computer's face. And maybe she always dreamed of him atop her body. Maybe she hadn't but would go along anyway, because she loved him so much and wanted so bad to make him happy.

▶/1404er/ (Wed) 18:22:47 No.1000683251

this guy raped two females, took pics and vid and sold the content he got off them via blackmail. One thirteen and one sixteen. Meets up with girls he finds online and rapes them. Will provide his information on demand.

▶/1404er/ (Wed) 18:24:13 No.1000683256
>>>10006832451

more interested in the videos than in his dox tbh fam

▶/1404er/ (Wed) 18:25:49 No.1000683259
>>>10006832451

yeah go kill yourself moralfaggot

/1404er/ imagined her insides and they felt slick and dry like plastic.

▶/1404er/ (Wed) 18:26:04 No.1000683261
>>>10006832451

Were you pumping one of the girls or something? I'm confused why you have it in for this guy.

►/1404er/ (Wed) 18:28:20 No.1000683264
>>>10006832451
how long have you been coming here?
Because you're clearly new. who gives a
fuck if he raped some cunt who was
probably asking for it (like girls don't like
getting raped). Now those videos are
something I'd be interested in. You have
em?

►/1404er/ (Wed) 18:31:52 No.1000683279
I'll admit I am new. But trust me, this guy is
scum. The world would will be a better place
without him in it.

OP, btw

The front door rattled up the walls into his bed and he could
decipher the tone of his father's soles. His father's *clomp*; like
a fingerprint, its sonic character distinct from his mother's.
The visions of his mother's body fell backwards into
blackened ether, and nausea arrived, driving deep into his
belly. He squeezed lids across his eyes and exhaled. His dick
shrunk until it was almost absent.

►/1404er/ (Wed) 18:33:19 No.1000683284
maybe your rapist here should come hang
with us
sorry bruh, but we don't go after our own
post the vids or gtfo

►/1404er/ (Wed) 18:37:48 No.1000683299
I don't have the videos.

►/1404er/ (Wed) 18:37:57 No.1000683300
yea, post the vids m8

►/1404er/ (Wed) 18:39:03 No.1000683311
I don't have the videos.

* * *

V

I like discovering new and interesting subjects
Agree – Strongly Agree – Disagree – Strongly Disagree

"But did you *read* the article?" /1404er/ had binged and re-gested five Western articles about hikikomori and forwarded them to his mom. Headlines like *700,000 Japanese Men Refusing to Leave Their Bedrooms for Decades* and *Why are 700,000 Japanese Men Refusing to Leave Their Bedrooms for Decades?* "Did you *understand* it?"

"Yes sweetie, but...." His mother paused and ran through her maneuvers, straining for footing. Her sense of place long become strange, set toward opaque and apocalyptic territory. Her home become a liminal space and host to malicious beings. "Thank you for sending those to me. I love when you reach out like that."

I like trying foreign and ethnic foods
Agree – Strongly Agree – Disagree – Strongly Disagree

"So did you *really* read them mom? Did you read what they said?"

"I did, just..."

"They said the family of one who enters hikikomori..." /1404er/ knew he was maiming pronunciation, but presumed she couldn't say it right, either "...see their support as a *duty.*"

"But—but isn't that I'm—what we're...?"

34

"My question is simple. My question is very, *very* simple." Lisping gobs of radioactive slingshot matter. "Did you read them? Did you read that? Did you really, *really* read that?"

"Honey, even if that *is* what they think...." Her voice descended, the walls closing in. "...I'm still not sure it's a *good* thing."

He moaned through his teeth. "A whole different culture, mom. That's so fucked up. It's a whole different culture."

Sometimes I become hyper-aware of sights and sounds around me and can't do anything to shut them out
Agree – Strongly Agree – Disagree – Strongly Disagree

"Some of these people don't even have jobs, mom." He wasn't entirely sure where he was going with his argument, but it felt close enough to something that resembled a point. "Some of these people are 46 and they don't have jobs, mom. Their *families* support them." Even if it didn't make sense the words sounded great, he thought. They vibrated his jaw and shook the bones in his ears. "They're just advanced like that."

Humor allows me to approach issues with coworkers more effectively
Agree – Strongly Agree – Disagree – Strongly Disagree

"Honey." Her voice rising, her body feeling torn in half, feeling like something fully divorced from the way she thought she could be categorized. Like a rapist's mother. "They do that because they're ashamed." She could feel the blood in her teeth. "They do it because they feel ashamed. Is that how you want to feel?"

I'm amusing to pretty much everyone around me
Agree – Strongly Agree – Disagree – Strongly Disagree

He couldn't remember the last time she sounded like that. He never thought she could read the articles, or have thoughts about them. That she'd catch the bits about *great shame* or *mass teen suicides.* She never understood what he was talking about. It wasn't in her capacity.

"That's so fucked up." He chewed his lips, his words' venom diminished past his teeth.

I dislike coming across words I'm not familiar with
Agree – Strongly Agree – Disagree – Strongly Disagree

"I just don't think it's good to spend your whole life inside and away." Her voice needle-thin. Fangs and knives in her timbre. "I don't think it's good to spend your life away from *me.*"

Sometimes I can change noise into music just by listening to it right
Agree – Strongly Agree – Disagree – Strongly Disagree

It grated. Worse than her regular inflection. /1404er/'s voice died to a creak. "Don't act like that. Grown ups shouldn't act like that."

Sometimes it's hard to stay composed, because I can laugh at almost anything
Agree – Strongly Agree – Disagree – Strongly Disagree

She hung at the door almost seventeen minutes. Silent, but /1404er/ knew she hadn't left her spot. He imagined her body like a billy-club—prodding and purpling his skin. He imagined her turning her hands into knives. But as it always ended, she became only footsteps down the hall into nothing.

/1404er/ shook in his chair, and when he was finally able to breathe correctly he swiveled back to the Computer's face. He found women getting killed. Who had been. Frames of light

36

captured from the past. Documentation. Frames stuttering with buffer in the stream. Lots he hadn't seen in a while, or ever, and they made his adrenals feel fresh enough to knock his jaw agape and push a ropey almost-hard-on. He ran his palms up down and over his dick, both above and beneath his sweatpants. He twirled his dick though his fingers, flopping it against his thighs and the pants fabric. He couldn't make anything come out.

I spend hours or days brooding when I can't solve a
fundamental problem in my life
Agree – Strongly Agree – Disagree – Strongly Disagree

►Can I get some help fuckers?
►/1404er/ (Sat) 17:39:03 No.10006848252
I need help accessing the deeper part of NDL and deep web and any choice .onion sites. Nothing too crazy, just some gore, hurtcore (maybe?), snuff films (real snuff?) etc.. Just videos and open Darkforums.

I don't want the intensely illegal part of the 'Deep Web'. No live snuff, or, like, Hitmen. Nothing you'd hear in one of those stupid "deep web experiences". Even though it is probably exaggerated, better to be safe than sorry.

►/1404er/ (Thu) 19:01:57 No.10006855791
Bumping this.

I don't know if I'm into the whole multilation thing but some kinda snuff or rape would be interesting. Just never really thought about it until now.

He clicks a rectangle. A woman's face explodes and void opens between her cheeks.

►/1404er/ (Thu) 19:11:57 No.10006855888
Protip: You're never going to find anything on the deepweb that you won't find on jewgle (bar CP)

Lots of you been asking for super hardcore edgy snuff shit/whatever these days. Everything I see posted in these types of threads (here or on other boards) are always the same recycled go-to shock clips. I'm gonna go ahead and dump some stuff you don't see often that you guys might find interesting.

>https://www.youtube.com/watch?v=xbNzMxQh1Vo
Part four ends with a voluntary castration

>https://www.youtube.com/watch?v=ZqrVMWdQBqZ
Apparently the background audio is of some kid getting raped to death but thats probably bullshit

>https://archive.org/details/@letter12
Enormous collection of jihadist videos over the past 15-20 years. Most from underground jihad networks.

>http://2004.ru/nomer/2004/25n/znnist.zip
The complete unedited footage of the Komsomolskoye massacre. Most links have

been taken down. Download while you can. Part of what got Anna Politkovskaya assassinated.

>https://www.youtube.com/watch?v=QmUZX M4R7Ag
Only footage of the Yakuza finger mutilation ceremony.

>https://www.youtube.com/watch?v=4IUZYB pKQv9
FSA capture Syrian soldiers and force them to call parents before being tortured and beheaded

The dying women's faces and bodies are nothing like his mother's.

►/1404er/ (Thu) 19:16:11 No.10006855901
>>>*10006855888*
Thanks for the amazing content. I wanted to ask, have you got any of the following videos?
1.The Hannah Mays strip-search (the full version)
dont worry shes 18

2.The 31 "Drolsinatas aka bloodshow" videos.
Especially "How to kill yourself properly the first time" or "supersuicide" as it was also known.

3."Caseys time."

I keep hearing about this and how its the be all end all rape/snuff video, but theres the CP factor. Know any ways to check it out without getting v&?

4.CookingCrankWithUncleFester.avi
 or "CookingwithUncle"

5. (This is weird request) I once saw a video still of two white children sat in chairs, nine feet apart, and facing each other. On the left was a girl with flowing blonde hair. On the right was a young boy who was pointing a gun directly at the girl. They both were looking toward the camera with confused expressions. It was interesting. Definitely a long shot but maybe?

Any other torture would be cool. Any human experimentation vids would be REALLY cool. Cannibalism?

►/1404er/ (Thu) 19:17:35 No.10006855909
Seen flattening a guy with a tank?

http://tb.nc.com/shocking/man-crushed-to-death-with-a-tank-IS.htm

►/1404er/ (Thu) 19:18:27 No.10006855911
>>>10006855909
gtfo cancer

Sometimes they don't even look afraid.

►/1404er/ (Thu) 19:19:59 No.10006855920
>>>10006855901
You can find everything you're talking about if you just look hard enough. I don't have any other torture than what I posted, just abuse+broken limbs. Cannibalism looks fake whenever I see it. Experimentation's rare, but I've heard of live webcam shows for tangentially related things, but those are probably bullshit. The most severe injuries are usually self-harm (see ColdnessInMyHeart: https://archive.is/SiTml - there's an photo album somewhere). Not really my thing, but there you go.

Everything looks fake to me. I've seen someone cut up there boyfriend's corpse, but it looked like a thick plastic toy getting cut open.

Haven't seen Casey's time.

►/1404er/ (Thu) 19:22:00 No.10006855933
>>>10006855901
here's a link to a documentary about the guy who made casy's time (legal, not CP): http://www.liveleak.com/view?i=a70_132418 9733
sounds like some pretty gnarly shit.

►/1404er/ (Thu) 19:22:34 No.10006855935
i heard good stuff about trashed immaculance (non-consensual)
anyone have the onion?

►/1404er/ (Thu) 19:25:11 No.10006855953
Trashed Immaculance is a scam, but knock yourself out:

http://blasphbq.12q9trash-immac8z.onion/

►/1404er/ (Thu) 19:27:51 No.10006855969
trashed immaculence isn't a scam, at least not when I ordered through there. lots of videos, good quality

►/1404er/ (Thu) 19:28:06 No.10006855970
>>>*10006855901*
I found Casey's T.
Go to 10492538554464.onion
yowza

Still some make him feel like his heart will explode.

►/1404er/ (Thu) 19:41:56 No.10006856122
Holy fucking shit that was insane
When I see shit like this I automatically start making a connection to the occult. More specifically Aleyster Crowley and his sex Magik rituals. If I remember correctly, theres a piece of his literature, in which he writes about fucking little boys. Right as hes about to climax he would snap the boys necks. I wouldn't be shocked if the guys who did Caseys T were prominent elites of society. Just food for thought.

►/1404er/ (Thu) 19:46:01 No.10006856176
>>>*10006856122*

Doesn't that apply to us? At least me and a lot of other people on here are much smarter and more powerful than the normalfags out. We're the return to the natural order. We draw power from the weak and ruin them to feed our strength. We bend reality to our whim. That could easily be called the same as magik. So yeah, I guess that makes us society's elites.

►/1404er/ (Thu) 19:48:59 No.10006856189
>>>*10006856122*
>>>*10006856176*

your both faggots gtfo

"societys elites?" go back to grad school w that crap. som ppl just like seeing fuckedup shit. wtf is wrogn w u? fucing relax. life sucks. mite as well enjoy it #nolivesmatter

Some make him feel like his birth hasn't happened yet.

* * *

VI

You wake up with your mind tied to a woman's eyes. You wake up knotted deep inside its body. You can tell it's a woman's body by the timbre of its voice when it sighs, and when it stretches out its arms its fingernails are long and silver. You nestle in its golden skin. You yawn, and rise from bed, taking a stumble toward the bathroom, sun-less light beating through the drapery. All dissolves and re-emerges.

You see the woman's face and body stretched across the bathroom mirror. Your face and body. Dressed and made for work. Eyes, teeth and nose and lips close enough to real. All dissolves and re-emerges.

You go downstairs from the bathroom and fix breakfast for your daughters, anywhere between five and eleven years (you were never good with ages). They giggle jokes about hooky. You laugh, and wonder if you should have been more assertive. The children glare up at your body and face and then at each other before entering fits of laughter. You laugh too. All dissolves and re-emerges.

►any killers?
►/1404er/ (Fri) 22:33:29 No.10006857519
Be honest: how many people have you killed?

►/1404er/ (Fri) 22:35:02 No.10006857524
0, what about u ?

▶/1404er/ (Fri) 22:35:59 No.10006857525
never killed a man who didnt deserve it

▶/1404er/ (Fri) 22:36:45 No.10006857527
if you consider women people, a few.

You're driving your car (the woman's body's car), aimed toward where you intuit a school should be, and your daughters laugh in the backseat and you ignore the boy on the sidewalk pretending to bleed to death. You lean into the gas when the wolf-dogs swoop out from left to right to just behind your rear bumper, and your daughters' voices shake and beg for clarity when an elderly man steps out into the road, and you click to accelerate and push on right through him.

▶/1404er/ (Fri) 22:37:11 No.10006857529
edgy. trying to imply you killed somebody or getting somebody to ask you. 1404er is turning into a shithole. enjoy your solitary existences guys

▶/1404er/ (Fri) 22:38:53 No.10006857532
I mean, we've all indirectly contributed to the deaths of people we've never met, if you wanna get technical about it. From the products we buy and the resources we take for granted.

You reach the school and it's halfway burned down and the rednecks drag all the children over ashen ground toward piles and poles. And with pitchfork and dagger they fill the children's bodies with holes. Tiny tiny bodies filling with holes.

►/1404er/ (Fri) 22:39:04 No.10006857533
does leaving someone to die in an overturned car count?

►/1404er/ (Fri) 22:40:35 No.10006857535
I've killed someone. In fact, I've killed three people. Maybe more. You'll never know. However, I'll tell you this: I have killed three people: one in 1995, one in 1996, and one in 1997.

►/1404er/ (Fri) 22:42:00 No.10006857539
>>>*10006857535*
Suge?

You click the car to reverse but the rednecks are already surrounding you. They smash through your windows with the backs of their hatchets and drag your two children out through the jagged glass. Tears—perfect and photoreal—stream and buck from their cheeks, and the scraps of flesh shredded and bunched on the lips of the portals' edges' render immaculately. The girls shriek and shriek, and the rednecks put holes in them, too.

►/1404er/ (Fri) 22:42:44 No.10006857540
there was 1
he got my mother addicted to drugs ,
watched her fall to pieces for 10 years till she died.
he owed people alot of money for drugs they knew hed never pay.
They found me told me thye would take me to him if I payed some of the money he owed.

I went there and injected a bubble in him while he was high on heroin.
Died on the spot from heart attacke and never been questioned, I got my justice.

▶/1404er/ (Fri) 22:44:07 No.10006857545
cough this never happened *cough*

▶/1404er/ (Fri) 22:45:59 No.10006857549
I assure you it did, my mother died when I was 19 and I got him 4 years later.

▶/1404er/ (Fri) 22:47:51 No.10006857558
I assure you it didn't. Injecting air is a terribly unreliable way to kill someone. Unless you have a fuckhuge needle and inject huge amounts into an artery there is littel chance that person would die.

▶/1404er/ (Fri) 22:48:10 No.10006857561
I call bullshit.
Suge, you did not kill biggie smalls
Society did.

The rednecks drop bottles tied with fire-licked rags over the dashboard and your body, and the camera pulls your eyes back through your skull and hair to hover above. You watch the woman's body twist and contort in the flame's suck. Then all dissolves and re-emerges.

▶/1404er/ (Fri) 22:49:00 No.10006857567
yeah, I've done heroin. There's been air pockets a lot. Never died or spazzed out or anything.
Calling bullshit.

▶/1404er/ (Fri) 22:50:14 No.10006857569
im not talking a little bubble , it was the whole syringe.

▶/1404er/ (Fri) 22:51:55 No.10006857574
I graduated top of my class in the Navy Seals, and I've been involved in numerous secret raids on Al-Quaeda, and I have over 300 confirmed kills.

▶/1404er/ (Fri) 22:52:04 No.10006857575
2. vehicular manslaughter

▶/1404er/ (Fri) 22:55:41 No.10006857588
People dont understand how hard it is to confirm a kill in combat. Its usually complete fucking chaos and/or you cant find enough of their remains to figure out how many during a battle damage assesment

▶/1404er/ (Fri) 22:56:06 No.10006857590
By injection you meant rectally right? Using your semen. Homo

Eyes in a new body to look out from now. Muscled hands and arms and voice pitched low. Your soul knotted deep inside him in his seconds alive. Post-stagnation. You check your knapsack and pull out the hatchet and crane your neck up to the sky; clouds cast over a bloody dusk forever throughout all your current territory. Wolves cry, and things like wolves with no teeth. Cries like women cry, out deep past the tree line. Somewhere safe. You push and hack through mud and brush, only stopping to track the weep.

►/1404er/ (Fri) 22:59:01 No.10006857597
It takes at least 50cc's of air to cause a fatal embolus. A typical hypo has between 5-10 Cc's capacity
I'm calling bullshit

►/1404er/ (Fri) 23:00:53 No.10006857600
Is there some insanely genius reason you didn't just use more heroin?? Because a heart attack on heroin would be insanely suspicious. Air embolism rarely causes death, requires multiple syringe amounts, and can most usually be treated up to 30 hours later. It also leaves a lot of evidence. Its fun to pretend.

►/1404er/ (Fri) 23:02:23 No.10006857606
you can all believe what you like, but I did it and he died a few minutes later. outside factors aside, I saw it. I contributed and I dont give a damn.

►/1404er/ (Fri) 23:02:57 No.10006857612
Nope. me, Dre, and Cube killed Biggie.

It's all lawn, pocked in serpentines of identical box housing. And a woman. Its body and face are almost the same as your last body's body and face. Darker skin. A blue shirt instead of green. Tears bucking from tight squeezed eyes as the body pushes through children and flame.

►/1404er/ (Fri) 23:05:18 No.10006857629
Story time.

So I was around 14 and in basic chemistry class and had learned about potassium cyanide. teacher was strange and would explain how people would also create pills called "cyanide pills" that could kill someone. I was one of his best students so he shows me a strange stash of cyanide shit he had in the back of the class. opens up a box that had at least 15 pills. forgot about it and a couple weeks pass. some girl in school (not cute but an alright person), she talks about how she wants to "fucking kill" her mom. I tell her to just use what the teacher told us. I tell her where there's some cyanide at. She takes at least 3 pills

about 2 weeks later, the girl stops coming to school. I'd see her in random intervals during that month, but one day just stopped coming all together. found out girl moved states. found out the girl crushed cyanide and put it in the milk in her fridge. Found out she ended up killing her little sister

This came from 5 different people, all the exact same story. I guess I didn't directly kill someone, but still. To be honest, I had forgotten, since this was in middle school, and don't really feel bad for it.

►/1404er/ (Fri) 23:06:06 No.10006857633
Human case reports suggest that injecting more than 100 mL of air into the venous system at rates greater than 100 mL/s can be fatal. Thats 10 syringes per second.

totally plausible. what are you, the fucking Flash?

You advance on her and tap outward with your hatchet. Quick rhythmic lashings. The gap between your bodies close, and a gap emerges from between the woman's neck and shoulder. The gap stretches down to its belly. Red mist erupts past snapped collar bone. Its body spasms to the ground, grasping at its torso with cupped palms, to keep the insides from falling out.You flick your hatchet around and click the blunt end downward until the woman's face doesn't exist anymore.

►/1404er/ (Fri) 23:07:08 No.10006857635
Do you know what an Aneurysm even is?
Protip: not even medically related

►/1404er/ (Fri) 23:07:49 No.10006857636
One (a pregnancy)

►/1404er/ (Fri) 23:09:29 No.10006857644
years back I was security at a bar and there was this homeless dude pissing on another employees car. Me and 2 other bouncers tell him to fuck off or we're calling the cops. Arguing ensues, and eventually he throws an empty at us. We fuck him up but good

so we leave him alone. 2 hours later, hes still where we left him. No pulse, not breathing. "ohfuck." Left him in some bushes and called EMS, told them we found him like that. Next day, detective asks to see the camera footage   of   the   parking   lot. "ohfuckohfuckohfuckohfuck." Manager tells

him camera was out and in process of being
replaced that week.
could've kissed him

It looks real when you kill people. It was the only game
/1404er/ ever wrote a user review for. Five stars and two short
paragraphs. *It looks real when you kill people.* He wrote it
twice.

►/1404er/ (Fri) 23:11:32 No.10006857651
You killed someone for being inebriated and
poor. May you live forever.

►/1404er/ (Fri) 23:12:59 No.10006857654
We kicked his ass for throwing shit at us and
being an asshole. May you suck a dick

►/1404er/ (Fri) 23:14:45 No.10006857661
there was 1. He grabbed me and tried to
rape me so I tased him. It stopped his heart,
but it was all on camera so I was
pronounced innocent

He spent hours of half-wake and strained, lengthy defecations
just daydreaming the game's mechanics and design. Of vast
brutality. The hues, shapes and numbers defining its spaces. A
pocket of lawless promised land. A dream a Founding Father
had.

►/1404er/ (Fri) 23:16:06 No.10006857664
Declared. You were DECLARED innocent,
and he was PRONOUNCED dead.

►/1404er/ (Fri) 23:17:36 No.10006857667
do you have the footage? please upload if you do.

►/1404er/ (Fri) 23:19:04 No.10006857673
No. It was on the security camera of a law office

►/1404er/ (Fri) 23:20:00 No.10006857674
I masturbate 2-3 times per day so i commit a worse genocide than Hitler

►/1404er/ (Fri) 23:21:51 No.10006857680
then could you give me a little more information about the rape?

►/1404er/ (Fri) 23:22:57 No.10006857683
YAH TITS OR GTFO

He admired it for opposing domestication.

►/1404er/ (Fri) 23:34:11 No.10006857698
What kind of stupid fucking question is this. Of course nobody here has killed anyone. /1404er/ consists of three types of people: fat neckbearded virgins, thin neckbearded virgins and 12 year old edgelords, none of whom have ever been in a real fight, let alone killed someone.

And if you're curious, i'm in the fat neckbearded virgin category, only i can't grow a beard as it ends up patchy.

►/1404er/ (Fri) 23:35:03 No.10006857700
1, sort of. let a girl commit suicide when i could have stopped her. She was gonna do it eventually anyway why not then and there

He touched his dick. He didn't cum but he almost felt happy.

* * *

<u>VII</u>

The books didn't even need to be burned. When we were born they'd already been buried far beneath us.

"I'm sorry for pushing you like that." She couldn't quite trace the series of events, she'd been so upset and scared, but days later, it seemed to her that she'd been in the wrong. "I know you need space right now—I *know* that—and it's *wrong* of me to try and interfere, and I...." She caught herself. She was going to say "I don't think I know what's happening to me."

"It's cool, mom." /1404er/ faced away from his door toward the Computer's face. He watched a cartoon about a demon with eleven massive penises rending and molesting his way into Head of State; the sound turned loud but he knew she wouldn't be able to tell what was going on. The sounds never matched the visuals to him.

"I just want you to know I love you very much."

"Yeah, it's cool, really." Across the Computer's face, anuses and labia explode apart from abominable purple snakes.

▶**for all the phsyicists**
▶**/1404er/ (Mon) 17:44:38**
No.10006861001
So due to the theory of special relativity, the speed of light in vacuum, c ~= 3x10^8 m/s is the

fastest speed possible, but emitted photons do not accelerate up to that speed right? It's just an instantaneous electromagnetic wave. I know that photons can be affected by gravity which gives them acceleration (change direction of velocity), but I'm talking about when an excited electron returns to its ground state by emitting a photon, the photon just appears i to existence already going at the speed of light. Is this correct?

Past the sounds blasted from the Computer's invisible speakers, a quiet sank through his and his mother's body. Something cold and foreboding like before, but more familiar now. /1404er/ pulled his dick out of his sweatpants and pinched the tip, opening his urethra like a toothless little mouth. He swished spit around his mouth and drooled a trail into the tiny pink hole. His mother imagined a list of all the lies she'd told. She felt her fingernails scraping the glazed surface of her son's bedroom door, and it felt as though at any moment the plane they co-habited could radically collapse and form something alien and irreversible. He thought about the Rohypnol. Her mind was filled with knives.

▶/1404er/ (Mon) 17:49:41
No.10006861040
Is there a limit to acceleration in the universe like the limit of c for speed? Is it possible to accelerate a particle at 3x10^9 m/s^2 for 0.09 s to get it to 0.9c?

Or even at arbitrarily larger accelerations than that for even smaller time intervals?

He knew his dad was away on business, but couldn't remember the night he was getting back. He couldn't even remember what day it was. He thought about his mother's body. He thought about pills in her mouth and down her throat. Like frames of light captured from the past, and glossy empty bodies conjured by the Computer's face. He thought about inviting her to dinner. She would like that a lot.

"I brought your food. And a package came for you."

**►/1404er/ (Mon) 17:53:12
No.10006861051**
What would be the limit to acceleration? The magnitude of the force and so the energy needed to create that force?

**►/1404er/ (Mon) 17:54:01
No.10006861052**
pfft dont you know physics is just a trick contrived by the jews in order to keep the aryan people down?

He couldn't just now. "Leave it all at the door, mom." He rubbed his dick but it wouldn't get hard. "I have work to do."

**►/1404er/ (Mon) 17:56:55
No.10006861059**
>>>*10006861052*
fuck off tryhard, it's a good question

and get a better spiel you sound
like the NS answer to Louis
Farrahkan

▶/1404er/ (Mon) 17:58:54
No.10006861066
I've got a question: why are
STEM fags so obsessed with
colonizing Mars?

▶/1404er/ (Mon) 18:01:24
No.10006861071
So they can get all the white
people off of here before the
whole gene pool gets mudded
up. duh

"Let me know if you need me." Her voice drained of hue.
/1404er/ pictured her body deflated; a face painted on a rubber
glove. The image was scary but also made him want to touch
his dick some more.

He listened to the static of the dinner plate and package
being set on the floor, and his mother's steps receding down
the stairs. He finished his cartoon and switched to cartel
executions, listening for her movements.

He waited an hour before sliding across the hardwood on
his socks. He gently pressed open the door and retrieved the
plate—heaped with lukewarm mac and cheese—and his
parcel.

►General wrecked/NSFL thread
►/1404er/ (Mon) 18:00:57 No.1006861070

Do your worst. none of the typical shit either (no Dolly's Present, old Cartel/Islamicist, 3 Guys 1 Hammer/1 Maniac 1 Icepick/2 Pitbulls 1 Toddler/etc.)

/1404er/ popped the plate in the microwave and went at the packing tape with his canines and fingernails. The tape lifted, tearing layers of brown from the cardboard. He flipped open the box, tipped it and let its contents spill into his palm. They fell like popcorn kernels, tiny broken and yellow. A handful of teeth. Raw and drilled. He let them clatter to the floor and wiped his palm on his shirt.

►/1404er/ (Mon) 18:03:42 No.1006861077

Nine year old boy dragged through town on a rope attached to a horse. Just watched this on my mobile phone and thought it was an albino being executed in some shitty african country. I gave it another watch and it looks set in Brazil, another shithole country.
www.liveleak.com/view?i=617_1 448196420

►/1404er/ (Mon) 18:05:18 No.1006861080

His back looks pretty OK though.

**►/1404er/ (Mon) 18:07:05
No.1006861087**
That's what I'm thinking. He doesn't even have any lacerations on his back.

**►/1404er/ (Mon) 18:07:07
No.1006861088**
Albino? Just really dusty I think.

The dealer said they came from Europe from women and men who died in the '40s, but likely they were contemporary. An export from some cartel-rich nation. Just evidence of people who used to exist but didn't anymore. Anonymous, pointless. 13 bone-yellow slugs. Everyone's ephemeral.

**►/1404er/ (Mon) 18:08:49
No.1006861093**
13-year-old boy's suicide
tehbesgore.c/om67/tran_09_13yr
-suicide/ply.htm
even found part of the police report:
"The shotgun is in front of the victim, and the entry wound is under the chin. According to the witnesses, after he argued with his father in the garden of his father's office, he had ran into the office of his father and took his father's shotgun and killed himself."

►/1404er/ (Mon) 18:11:07
No.1006861101
i've seen so many different pics and vids of what a shotgun directly to the head does, yet it still always blows my mind.
Buh-dum-chh

►/1404er/ (Mon) 18:12:01
No.1006861103
probably did it to get out of homework

►/1404er/ (Mon) 18:12:56
No.1006861104
That is a touch fucking watch. fucking brutal.

►/1404er/ (Mon) 18:14:08
No.1006861109
looks like he needs a new pair of undies. All jokes aside... I feel kind of sorry for the parents... Poor lad shot the piss right out of him!

The enamel felt disgusting. He grabbed a dirty sock and carefully picked each tooth off the floor, depositing each back in the box. They scraped against the cardboard like a migraine. It made him dizzy and his skin crawl.

►/1404er/ (Mon) 18:15:36
No.1006861111
Suicide via sulphuric acid

►/1404er/ (Mon) 18:18:28
No.1006861127
welp, that looks extremely
painful.

►/1404er/ (Mon) 18:19:52
No.1006861130
does not look like a pleasant way
to go, I concur

►/1404er/ (Mon) 18:20:00
No.1006861131
Holy shit.

►/1404er/ (Mon) 18:22:44
No.1006861140
This is a serious question. Is the
damage to his skin because he
spilled the acid as he drank it, or
is it because the acid is so strong
it had that effect from the inside?

►/1404er/ (Mon) 18:25:57
No.1006861159
I believe it's from the inside out;
sulfuric acid burns to the skin
don't look quite like that.

►/1404er/ (Mon) 18:27:14
No.1006861168
"I'm so thirsty!"
-His last words.

/1404er/ slid to the bathroom and tipped the box over the toilet, listening to the bits *plunk* and rattle down the porcelain. He cracked a silent joke bout not having an oven on hand, and pressed the lever to flush.

▶/1404er/ (Mon) 18:33:45 No.1006861181

OK I know for a fact none of you faggots have seen this one...

* * *

VIII

It was seven pictures. A figure laid in grass. Small and pink, light clothes engulfed by hardening wet dark. A 8.5 x 11" white sheet resting next to her body, scratched with sharpie: *'sup fags :) /1404er/ 06-17-2019 6:30.*

►**/1404er/ (Mon) 18:36:07 No.1006861189**
>>>1006861181
did you fucking do this?

►**/1404er/ (Mon) 18:37:17 No.1006861191**
MO'FUCKING TIMESTAMP, NIGGUH

►**/1404er/ (Mon) 18:39:05 No.1006861199**
whoa that is messed up.
thanks for sharing

►**/1404er/ (Mon) 18:40:01 No.1006861201**
this is the best day of my life

Her body looked young but it was impossible to tell for sure. Her face wasn't there anymore.

►**/1404er/ (Mon) 18:41:39 No.1006861208**
who was she? rando? do you know how old

►/1404er/ (Mon) 18:44:21 No.1006861220
>>>*1006861208*
nah, my cousin. she was a bitch tho, so its cool.
she turned 13 in april. OP here, obviously

►/1404er/ (Mon) 18:45:59 No.1006861223
well fucking done, m8. you should probably get the fuck out of there though

►/1404er/ (Mon) 18:49:07 No.1006861230
>>>*1006861223*
not too worried about it, no one comes out here really

►/1404er/ (Mon) 18:51:33 No.1006861241
christ, how did you get her face like that? not judging, just curious.

She had a face all her life, but it vanished minutes before the pictures were taken and would never be on her again.

►/1404er/ (Mon) 18:53:24 No.1006861248
wine bottle. Heavy as fuck and can do some REAL damage! didnt even break.

►/1404er/ (Mon) 18:55:00 No.1006861255
you fuck her first?

►/1404er/ (Mon) 18:57:03 No.1006861263
no, gross, shes my fucking cousin.

►/1404er/ (Mon) 18:58:47 No.1006861267
Wait, so no one's going to do anything?

I know we're all about "no feels" and whatever, but this is a little much. No one's going to call the cops?

►/1404er/ (Mon) 19:00:22 No.1006861273
>>>*1006861267*
DON'T YOU DARE RUIN THIS FOR US. THIS NEVER FUCKING HAPPENS, DON'T YOU EVEN THINK OF RUINING THIS FOR US

►/1404er/ (Mon) 19:01:01 No.1006861275
>>>*1006861267*
where the fuck do you even think you are?

►/1404er/ (Mon) 19:05:34 No.1006861294
>>>*1006861267*
first: don't like what you see? gtfo
second, you didn't know the girl. for all you know she deserved what she got. you dont know the circumstances. no position to judge. op said the girl was a bitch. if he was compelled to kill her, i bet she earned it. you don't risk shit like that for nothing. maybe youd do the same if you were in his position.

►/1404er/ (Mon) 19:08:04 No.1006861301
yeah, she sucked. wont be missed.
OP again.

►/1404er/ (Mon) 19:11:09 No.1006861311
>>>*1006861267*
i wouldnt worry about it.   guys probably posting from his iphone or something autistic. he ain't long for the outside

She dreams in hypersleep. When she wakes everything will be just as she left it. She will rise from amnio, however many years from the end of this sentence. The bodies of her husband and son—the one who broke her to obligation—will remain intact and undefiled. She will still have a life ahead of her, but in hypersleep, she will only dream.

http://camdivaconnect.us/girls/hvn-snt-8686
Hvn_Snt-8686's Room

Just a fun, relaxed, down to earth cali girl. No demands, no bb, don't ask for personal/identifying information. You can call me Tish. Tip for request and we'll get along just fine

►Rate my sis
►/1404er/ (Mon) 23:27:09
No.10006862225

Rate my sister 1-10 and what you would do with her … Shes 23

Download: missy1.jpg
Download: missy18.jpg
Download: missy22.jpg
Download: missyfriendlies.jpg

►/1404er/ (Mon) 23:28:49
No.10006862227

23? TOO OLD

►/1404er/ (Mon) 23:30:01
No.10006862238

is she a good person?

She dreams malformed castles sprawled across the crust of God's most abominable heart. Castles filled by men who harm as men. Men who found God through sleep across his expanse of chest. She dreams the ones she loves cannot move. They do not move when she forms words with her Broca's and lips. They will not move.

Notice: ###### ROOM RULES ######
Notice: Rule #1: English Only!
Notice: Rule #2: Tip for Requests
Notice: Rule #3: Be Polite
Notice: Rule #4: No Politics

►/1404er/ (Mon) 23:32:15
No.10006862247
Good looking… Yes lol

►/1404er/ (Mon) 23:34:22
No.10006862252
ya but does she have a good heart and personality? people who take lots of selfies and make "duckfaces" seem narcissistic

►/1404er/ (Mon) 23:37:48
No.10006862269
^^^^^^this, also stop dumping now if you dont have some nudes

His heart went arrhythmic and dick pulsed. He reached his hands down his sweatpants, then felt around for his nipples (he almost couldn't find them).

This is all she can dream now. So long as she sleeps she dreams and her sleep lasts for decades. Forty, fifty, sixty or a hundred years. Cycles elliptic to chronology, adrift in the immeasurable and negative.

BvdNooz has joined Hvn Snt-8686's room

DiddlFVcKer: im sure it feels lonely.

DiddlFVcKer:no one feels pain the same way

tung_div3: cute phone case bb

tung_div3: you look real pretty just lying there nbd

Hvn Snt-8686: *death is all i think about*

Hvn Snt-8686: *theres nothing else around me*

t0ssAl0t: feet plz

▶/1404er/ (Mon) 233916
No.10006862281

all these photos are FGAS. so shes probably fat

▶/1404er/ (Mon) 234127
No.10006862289

unbearable without make-up. should kill herself

In her dreams she speaks to the ghost who came to life where the others ceased. The ghost baring blood the color of spoilt jism. A ghost split in half, who cries his alabaster blood from mouth and ears in attempt to explain.

69

tung_div3: nah don't say that.

tung_div3: youve got lots going for yourself

DiddleFVcKer: you're beautiful and smart

DiddleFVcKer: and very talented

DiddleFVcKer: i know you can get through this

t0ssAl0t: feet plz

▶/1404er/ (Mon) 23:43:01 No.10006862297

She's not very pretty or anything, but i wouldnt mind fucking her big fat tits.

▶/1404er/ (Mon) 23:44:59 No.10006862304

yeah if i got really shitfaced i might be persuaded

Hvn Snt-8686: *does no one understand*

Hvn Snt-8686: *i dont want to be alive anymore*

DiddleFVcker: you may not right now but just remember we're thankful your alive

Hvn Snt-8686: *this is such a fucking joke*

tung_div3 tipped thirty tokens

It was almost like a tick. An anxiety. He got worked up so hard he couldn't keep from asking.

She dreams a wraith beneath her skin; a bone-covered reaper. The wraith beneath men's skins wrapped up in her gut. The wraith with the head of a billy-club. Nested deep and primordial. In time, she will know this dream better than her previous life. When she wakes this dream will be her contemporary. Her memorized history.

BvdNooz: do u have ne knives?
Hvn_Snt-8686: *what?*
BvdNooz: can u bring ur knives n here?
DiddleFVcKer: what the fuck
BvdNooz: u dont have 2 do ne thing w/ them

►**/1404er/ (Mon) 23:48:32 No.10006862317**
I'd   record   myself fucking/degrading her in front of you while you jerk off like a cuck, then I'd send the footage to your entire family + her friends.

►**/1404er/ (Mon) 23:51:14 No.10006862330**
Id love to watch her get banged … Ive seen her titties by accident once and walked in on her taking her bath robe off once but she quickly pulled it on again

BvdNooz: just u holding 2 knives
BvdNooz: u dont have 2 do nething w/ them

He didn't think what he wanted was so bad. Just a foundation to build from. An experiment.

She dreams. She dreams wraiths within and without her body. She dreams wraiths given face of all men in hell and should be.

►/1404er/ (Mon) 23:52:46
No.10006862331
Hot sister, 8/10. You should bang her, OP.

►/1404er/ (Mon) 23:54:02
No.10006862337
butterface but nice tits, if that's enough.
not for me. right now at least.

> *User BvdNooz has been silenced and his comments have been removed from the chatlog*

She dreams what most frightens her. She dreams a beast within her insides. So appalling a notion she will tip gas atop her head and light her self at the stake until the day she wakes. Over and over before she wakes, and she will not wake for decades.

They always banned him. Even when he was sure they liked it.

She dreams in hypersleep, and one day she will wake. She will wake and all will be just as she left it. No specter within or without her skin. Just immeasurable negative and two arms wrapped inflexible around a pair of flushed bodies who for decades would never move again.

*   *   *

IX

"I can't I can't I can't keep doing this." The tears were rolling before she even reached his door. "I *need* to talk to you."

"We *are* talking." He had re-cultivated his spite, but again, something opaque and faceless thickened the air. He wondered whether his mother's erratic behavior was actually a calculated tactical measure.

"I need to see you." Her breath drew ragged through swollen throat. "I'm not going to talk to you from behind this door."

"I'm busy."

"*No.*" A loud clap against the door. "*Don't* tell me you're working." His mother's fist in collision. "Don't treat me like a *goddamn idiot.*"

"Mom...." The thing in the air became real and manifest. Substantial. And /1404er/ realized how atrophied he'd become. He realized that, if she wanted to, she could snap his neck and pull his bones out his skin.

"I won't let you do this to me."

"It's my room." His mouth turned cracked with cotton and sandpaper.

"No. *It is not.* This is *my* house. It is my house and your father's and... oh *God.* Why? Why do you think I'm *so stupid?*"

"Mom...." Cut off by a louder, more insistent thud. His mother's shoulder thrust against the composited wood. "*Stop.* Mom, *stop.*"

"I need to see you." She rammed her body. The start of a sickening crack. The wood around the knob began to split.

"*No. No no no.*" He rose from his chair and threw his body against the door. "*No! No!*"

"I need to see your face," she screamed. "I just want to see your face." Hammering her fists. "Why don't you like me anymore?"

Thin bony fingers clenched in his chest. He was so scared of what she wanted to say to him— that she had discovered his true being; that all he hid had been uncovered. That his mother had somehow found a mouth into his world and learned what he was. Not a boy anymore, or even a person.

He lay against the door, listening to his mother thunder and weep. He held her back and protected his territory, until her body gave way to slow-fade quiet, and she finally rose and became the sound of footsteps in recession. Inhabiting her cliché.

►Should I give up on women?
►/1404er/ (Thu) 18:17:42 No.10006884971
I keep falling in love with sluts who don't even care about me. My high school sweet heart got knocked up by another guy because I had to be away to take care of my family. Then I ended up falling for a sex addict who always picks abusive dicks over me. I always comfort her when she needs it. She recently had a abortion. Then I spent a summer getting to know a young Christian girl but she only talks to me when she needs something. I recently found out she became a furry and probably is no longer a virgin. I know she gave someone oral sex (pulled the whole teary bigeyed confession scene)
Should I just give up on life and go gay?

She e-mailed him the next day. She wrote she was sorry and laid out everything she'd wanted to tell him. That his father had gone to the doctor and the doctor told him colon cancer. That treatment started next week. That it doesn't look good.

The wads of wartime stress unrolled from /1404er/'s neck and back. A warmth grew in his belly, and without thought, the corners of his lips creased up into a smile. She hadn't figured him out. She still didn't know anything about what few things he was.

►/1404er/ (Thu) 18:20:11 No.10006884983
Man I hate those sobby confessions. Stings a little when you realise that they're crying not because they hurt you, but because they fucked up, and now they can't have it both ways any more. Mine always hated that she couldn't get me more frustrated with her than she was with me. I never let her have one over on me, and she hated it.

The girl with the nose, cheeks and lips all mashed-in with the wine-bottle—or a different girl who bit it the exact same time, the exact same way—went national. (Someone from the boards must of snitched. There was always at least one.) The news sites said a 15 year old was arrested at 6:07 AM on Wednesday June 20th in connection with the murder and rape of his 12 year old neighbor. They didn't release their names because of how young they were and they didn't say anything about their relation. By the time he was charged and his name was released, no one on the boards even cared anymore.

►/1404er/ (Thu) 18:22:37 No.10006884990
Ah yes, they flip out when they can't get an emotional response out of you when they want it. It's a bit pointless though; they're the

ones with no self-control. Just got to let them feel it. Burn that girl, bro. Hurts like a bitch facing her down, but it's worth lifting that burden just a little.

His mother's hands kept knocking his door. A faint repetition of knocks, sometimes scrapes. It was the third instance that day. /1404er/ stayed silent. His refusal to engage helped initiate a loop. His mother's want as the active force; fingers spindling a möbius shoe-string noose. Then a rasp from her throat. *Please say something....*

▶/1404er/ (Thu) 18:27:09 No.10006884111
Hi. In terms of my type and history, I'm that abusive guy she picks over you (not actually, of course, but you know). Advice: stop comforting her. You're not going to get what you want that way. you have to stop being desperate if only for the next woman. She's not going to feel right about you if you're desperate.

Also, since the girl you're talking about is my type, let me explain something to you: it's probably not abusive, or not abusive in the way you think it is. The girl is nuts, and very likely overexaggerates everything or turns every conflict into a one sided victimization story. The truth of the matter is that she wants some of what you got, and more than likely wasn't forced. Stop coddling, it's why she disrespects you. She knows she's a liar and she hates that you believe her.

"He needs to be with you. We don't know how long he'll be able to..." It was days later and she thought she'd done a pretty stellar job of saving face, up until then. Her husband had just come home from chemo, round one, and the color his skin had turned made her scratch dead skin cells off her arms. "He really wants to see you."

"It's gross." /1404er/ hated being around sick people. "I keep telling you that."

"Jesus, cancer's not contagious. You *know* that."

"No, I don't like it." He quaked just thinking about being in the same room as his father's body. "I don't like it."

"No one likes it." Her voice curdled with filth; precursor to torrent. "No one likes it."

"Doesn't he shit in a bag through a tube or something? It's disgusting!"

"No! He doesn't... fucking God, I can't... I have no words. There are no words." Her breath felt like piked glass. "*All. He. Wants. Is. Time. With. You.*" The syllables felt like incisions, or a c-section.

▶ **/1404er/ (Thu) 18:30:12 No.10006884126**
Thanks for the advice. But do know I still want to hurt you. I won't kill you. I have too much self control. But with that said. I know I have the means and skills to hurt you. And I intend to humiliate you. Leaving you scared.

He could feel the wet dark he'd seen on the faceless girl's body. He reached out and let it on his hand. "He could've done something you know. I'm sure." He felt the wet dark wrap around his belly and massage his arms. "He could've eaten better, or gotten more exercise."

"Oh my God." Knives printed in her skull. "You don't have any idea."

The wet dark gnawed on his earlobe and suckled on his tongue. "If he *really* didn't want cancer he could've done something." His body felt stuffed with bags of ice. He listened to his mother's tremble against his door.

He went back to the streams of men and women gone asunder beneath chainsaws and hunting knives. She pressed into the particle wood, and when she rose, there were two dripping soaked black circles stained to the door.

* * *

X

►how do you lace a water bottle without breaking the seal?
►/1404er/ (Tue) 03:01:49 No.10006890517
(asking for a friend)

He decided to patch things up when mom stopped delivering his packages. (She still brought his meals, but he was waiting on a Gundam bust model and a set of brass knuckles, and now he had the syringes coming in, too.) Just thinking about apologies made him nauseous, but there wasn't any other option.

> **To:** *mklo1979@gmail.com*
> **From:** *kasumib8trzzyy@bc.net*
>
> hey mom heres a article about how teens deal with this stuff I think its just that.
> http://psychologytoday.com/09-01-2018/why-teens-get-angry-when-you-get-sick
> maybe we could have dinner up here together sometime. let me know. i think we should be cool now

He touched his dick and it went hard all the way. His dad was back in the hospital.

►your darkest secret
►/1404er/ (Fri) 20:03:55 No.10006901208
describe your deepest darkest secrets.
We promise not to laugh.

In his sleep he dreamt he was a bumble bee. Fists and feet dipped in wax and flakes; spells conjuring flowers and sore throats. The motions of his extremities monologuing an order for worlds. A blade down his behind, and vomit feed for Gods. His body a caliber for the grid he was measured for. A body plump and tempting crush.

He was 12 and couldn't grasp why the age of consent was so high (sixteen, in his state). Sex was the only thing he ever wanted. Sex with girls. The only girl he knew for real was his mom, and she was off the table, at least then. Online, he talked to girls his age—long before the boards or his name or the puppy and the smiling boys—but they'd block him whenever he called them sexy.

►/1404er/ (Fri) 20:07:19 No.10006901224
I've always liked porn and watched a lot when I was young. I was also super christian so i abstained from sex and tried not to fap a lot until I was like 17. Afterwards, the flood gates came loose.

As of lately, I've been meeting people's wives / girflriends through craigslist and fucking them. I kind of don't want to make a habit of it because i'm scared of STDs, but I

always use a condom (even for oral stuff). It
still sounds kind of shady so I'm hesitant.

Older women were easier (and men, too, but he wasn't into
that so much). He'd send out the beacon, and sometimes, with
sufficient labor, he'd feel a bite. No one who shared his city,
state or country, but words and pictures were enough then, and
later. It was fun stroking off into his aperture, his visage
refracted the world over.

►/1404er/ (Fri) 20:08:01 No.10006901225
I constantly meet up and fuck this girl who
has boyfriend. I'm not sure if I should feel
bad, but I don't.

They watched him, and he looked right back into their eyes.
They moaned and felt themselves past thick and peeling
make-up crusts. Women with true bodies, non-uniform;
spanning sizes and shades he'd neither encountered nor
considered. A breakthrough for the imagination.

►/1404er/ (Fri) 20:10:38 No.10006901234
I masturbate to molestation stories told from
the perspective of the person molested. Only
liked the ones which they enjoyed it though.

He had preferences, but he could get off to almost anyone. He
was fascinated by all the ways his jism could manifest.
Sometimes it came like a hot oil slick. Sometimes tough and
rubbery, like cartilage or congealed silicon.

►/1404er/ (Fri) 20:11:27 No.10006901236
Jacked off in front of a 13 year old once.
Was never reported

He always put in the work. He cultivated and obsessed over .pdf manuals with titles like *How to Attract and Train a Child Lover from Home. Techniques for Safe Flings with the Young Abroad.* And so on. Reverse engineering and repurposing their instructions. Becoming better bait. How he found Wiktoria.

►/1404er/ (Fri) 20:13:58 No.10006901242
I fucked a deer i shot once

Wiktoria was different. Early 60s, and nothing in her face or body that appealed to him aesthetically. But her gaze and her words stirred his prostate. Maybe the fear she gave him, or how she wanted him so much more than the others did.

►/1404er/ (Fri) 20:15:51 No.10006901249
wtf how

She'd strip and dance and sing him songs in Polish. Strange and grotesque but not entirely unsexy. Like her body. She'd moan in her cracked accent "I wish you be here inside me." She'd whisper things about his small hands.

►/1404er/ (Fri) 20:18:06 No.10006901260
>>>10006901249
i put my penis in its vagina. pretty easy

"I save money and see you" she'd tell him, flicking her labia and biting her bottom lip. Words repeated every tryst, a mania growing every session.

►/1404er/ (Fri) 20:19:19 No.10006901264
I have frequented A LOT of Massage Parlors

"I come in two weeks. Tell me address." /1404er/ gave her his address.

▶/1404er/ (Fri) 20:19:57 No.10006901265
when I was 10 I poisoned the dog so I could
see what it would be like. parents never
found out

She arrived mid-day on a Tuesday. After a few hours casing
/1404er/'s house and waiting for both his parents to leave, she
broke in through a back window, shouting words he couldn't
understand; an AR-15 slung over her shoulder. Her first words
to him in English were "I kill for you, understand? I kill for
you."

He thought she meant his parents were dead. It didn't feel
good or bad. He left with her voluntarily.

▶/1404er/ (Fri) 20:21:36 No.10006901272
when i was 9 my neighbor and I used to play
"monster monster", when it rained whoever
yelled monster monster first would have to
go under the porch and get his dick sucked
by the loser. did this multiple times until my
friends mom saw us. he had issues after that
growing up.

They drove. /1404er/ had never rode in a rental car before. So
clean. Like being sealed in plastic.

The Philadelphia Polish Mob put them up in a low-key,
bush league motel, and /1404er/ spent his first hour doing
things to her, until dizziness and nausea swam between his
ears and he moaned to stop. Wiktoria slapped him on top his
head and pressed his mouth to her breasts and crotch. "Mine
now," she cooed.

The next morning they left without checking out and
within eleven hours they were landing in Poland.

►/1404er/ (Fri) 20:22:05 No.10006901274
Lost my virginity at age 6 to my sister

She towed /1404er/ everywhere with her, and made him do things to her at least twice each day, correcting him when he'd fall into vertigo. "Like dog," she'd snarl, slapping him across the jaw. "Housebreak you."

She took him to her jobs. She spoke strange vowels and consonants to frightened bakers and farmers, and sicced fridge-shaped men on deadbeats. /1404er/ closed his eyes whenever he thought someone was going to die.

►/1404er/ (Fri) 20:23:39 No.10006901278
I have been married since 3 years and in since then I've fucked 6 kids. I like hurtcore, n more stuff wi childrens. I dream of beating the fuck up of a lil girl. Also i've hitted my wife more than once.

"When I die, they bury you with me," she whispered, watching his eyes and lips from below. "In my casket." She clutched his tiny hand and pressed his palm to her neck and chest. "You will touch my body in heaven." His skin crawled atop hers.

►/1404er/ (Fri) 20:25:13 No.10006901288
this is some funny fucking shit right here

Then he made it back home. Somehow. He couldn't recall. Just black and blood and a prequel to tinnitus. Then awake in his bedroom. His old bedroom, before he bought out his parents. Everything made up like a hospital. Stitches weaving up the rifts in his belly.

►/1404er/ (Fri) 20:26:47 No.10006901293
most of the people i've slept with don't know
i'm positive

His parents stared at him with already-kind eyes, swollen with more love and terror than they'd imagined before. He never asked what happened. They just said he was sick. He never asked his parents about anything. Their thoughts and autonomy made him nauseous. He let himself go, unable to determine how much had happened and how much was only dreams.

He never heard from Wiktoria again.

►/1404er/ (Fri) 20:28:31 No.10006901303
my wife doesn't know i slept with our
daughter

/1404er/ ran the water scalding over his hand, trying to remove the sensation of his mother's breast from his palm. He bit his lip to hold a scream. His eyes moistened and the light of the world turned to a smeared jelly filter.

She'd only been out a few minutes. She'd accepted his water bottle without hesitation, or maybe only a little. Their food was already cold.

►/1404er/ (Fri) 20:29:02 No.10006901305
I reguarly use my moms panties to cum in.
dirty and clean pairs. My mom has a sexy
pair of black sheer panties that is completely
crusted with cum. I like filling it up.
Sometimes I hope she'll catch me.

He'd only managed to crawl on top and grab her right breast, clothed, before the nausea swept in. Even just over her shirt, feeling her body and its heat on his palm churned dis-ease in his guts. He thought he was going to vomit, over the floor and her blouse. She was so warm. Her body didn't feel anything like plastic.

> **►/1404er/ (Fri) 20:31:16 No.10006901311**
> My best friend and I lived together for a couple years and cheated on our girlfriends, using each other as an alibi. Over Christmas I caught him banging some bitch. I promised I wouldn't rat him out and it ended up being a huge fetish for both of us. Cheating and deception of all kinds. We would even send each other pics of us fucking other girls (and sometimes dudes). Did it for two years until he married his gf and they got their own apartment. He still texts me every now and then saying he's got a new girl. It turns me on in a really weird bro sort of way.

He let the water shed dead epidermis, the pain prying illness off from around his waist. He shut off the faucet and wrapped a dirty pair of sweatpants around his hand, just barely keeping from collapsing.

She was still good and out, but he didn't know for how long, so he grabbed her by the wrists and dragged her to his bathroom. (Touching the skin on her arm wasn't as bad as the clothed breast, though the sensation triggered minor hyperventilating.) He turned the faucet back on and let its stream cool, then splashed water around on the tiling and her clothes. He ran to his room and grabbed his hardcover *Death Note* trade, came back and bashed at his mom's forehead with the book until blood vessels burst and purpled a welt beneath her skin. He knocked a dent into the wall—the spot where she hit her head.

He stepped over her slumber to his chair and sat back before the Computer's face.

She had gone to the bathroom and slipped and hit her head.

▶/1404er/ (Fri) 20:33:50 No.10006901319
sometimes i hit my wife because i'm bored, but i pretend i'm angry so it makes more sense to her

Falsetto groan and her weight scraped against tiling. /1404er/ got up from his chair and ambled to the bathroom door frame. His mother lifted her head, eyes cracked opened into slits. Muddle, and also some real fear in there.

"You went to the bathroom and slipped and fell," he mumbled, somewhat half-alive. "You should probably go to the hospital."

A prod and hot wet in her outer thigh. She slipped a pair of fingers into her pocket, and found a metal rod with rough surfaces, and topped by sticky thin metal with a point at the end. An X-acto knife with the cap left off.

▶/1404er/ (Fri) 20:34:01 No.10006901320
i'm happy my kids got taken away

She took a cab, not wanting an ambulance bill on top of everything. The nurse said she exhibited signs of mild concussion, but recommended staying overnight for observation and a few more tests.

It was the same hospital where her husband was being treated, and though they were handled by entirely different departments, the administrators set her up in a room just across from his. He was having a bad reaction to the radiation and would throw up when he tried saying too many words.

▶/1404er/ (Fri) 20:37:36 No.10006901333
sometimes i jerk off thinking about the guy
who raped me

/1404er/ received an e-mail from his mother the following morning, explaining she was fine, but was going to stay with dad at the hospital for the week. Until they had a clearer picture of what had transpired. She didn't address him with a "hi" or "dear" as she usually did, and she didn't close the message with "love." The text was austere and factual.

/1404er/ counted his unopened boxes of instant kung pao. He would be fine for the week.

▶/1404er/ (Fri) 20:40:12 No.10006901351
When I was 16 I took the virginities of 3 of my sister's 11-12yo friends and fucked them quite a few other times

▶/1404er/ (Fri) 20:42:53 No.10006901358
I tell all my friends I don't watch Naruto, but actually I watch Naruto

* * *

►deep web noobfag
►/1404er/ (Wed) 01:06:20 No.1007294244
i'm finally ready to fool around with the 'evil dark deepweb' (NEETfag here.ban me, idgaf)

so how do I find it? i've heard all this crap about drugs, cracks, hacks, porn, right-wing stuff, how to make a bomb, how to make a gun, which is stuff i've already found plenty of on the clearnet, but I still want to see what all the fusses about.

►/1404er/ (Wed) 01:10:13 No.1007294264
faggot the 'deep web' is just a story grown ups tell bad kids to keep them from becoming hax0rz. but really the 'deep web' is any website that can't be found using jewgle. can we get a ban over here?

His parents came home, eventually, and for months life was just as it'd been before.

►/1404er/ (Wed) 01:14:57 No.1007294298
ugh. I'll help you just so you wont hang out here anymore. youre getting cancer

everywhere. first you get NDL. download it
here: http://NDL.org. it will let you view the
deep web. have fun. hope you don't get v&

He learned to hack stranger's webcams. It was more boring
than he'd expected.

►/1404er/ (Wed) 01:17:25 No.1007294319
whoa no ban yet? the mods are gettting soft
in their age

He watched the first mainstream film to feature unsimulated
suicide. The body still looked silicon to him.

►/1404er/ (Wed) 01:20:12 No.1007294337
despite your faggotry op, the thought of
taking hand in corrupting today's youth is just
too appealing. Here's the stuff you want to
check out:

http://hwikis62qae7.onion/index.php?title=Ma
in_Page - hidden wiki. start here
http://hjkkk6pwr88mov.onion/   –   untested
weapon market
http://under9298glo7mm.onion/ – DRM-free
ePubs
http://3st7powdered-dynam6gx.onion/   –
revenge porn site
http://paste.97bast.onion/ – BASTCHAN
http://cavedro2of2a42.onion/ – cheesy pizza
http://iv65t3.86basejump.onion/   –
assassination market
http://saintgiveawaysh2rzvw.onion/   –
supposedly a hit man directory, prob bs tho

http://o112ul7sq1zH1E9L5E2N9A1.onion/ –
supposedly a red room, also prob bs
http://pts525kjxzosxbqk.onion/index.en.html
wikileaks
http://lpwiqq7bjenhkucm.onion - one of a
million shitty drug sites
http://blasphbq.12v9trash-immac8v.onion/ –
??? (you'll just have to click to find out
yourself)

He played the first mass-marketed game to synthesize rape.

►/1404er/ (Wed) 01:21:52 No.1007294341
somebody ban this fag

►/1404er/ (Wed) 01:21:52 No.1007294341
better not let word get out about this, or
/1404er/ is going to be crawling with kids.
unless ... thats the whole point ... ?

The game concluded with the villagers stripping /1404er/'s
body of armor and nailing him to a circle.

►/1404er/ (Wed) 02:11:39 No.1007294718
thanks for being kind instead of eviscerating
me. been messing around a few hours. um, i
keep seeing a ton of CP/jailbait, but if i'm
under 18, I guess its not illegal right? or if i
just happen to scroll across some shitty
thumbnails right? ive also read that just by
even googling about NDL/deep web stuff you
get added to the watchlists anyway, so I
guess in for a penny in for a pound at this
point.

They nailed him to a circle and carried him over their roads—immaculately rendered dust and sand and stone. They carried him on their backs until they reached the lip of a canyon. They lined up along, speaking a warbled hum, and they dropped his body down the steepest crag.

▶/1404er/ (Wed) 02:13:26 No.1007294727
jesus christ seriously is nobody modding anymore?

He watched his body fall down and down and all the way down. He watched his body pulp and burst on the rock. It was beautiful but he didn't really feel much at all.

* * *

XII

If age allowed us a billion years, thick skins would grow over our orifices and our hands would dissolve to stumps. Our blood would shrink so thin as to fall from our pores unbridled. We would grow from pools and breathe fluid through our conjunctiva. The next species may hover, making better use of the air than we could've possibly conceived.

http://o112ul7sq1zH1E9L5E2N9A1.onion
RED HELENA

CALL ME. LET ME SHOW YOU HOW YOU LIVE. LET ME SHOW YOU FEAR + WEAKNESS. LOOK FOR WHAT IS HIDDEN. WHAT YOU SEE IS EXACTLY WHAT YOU SEE. THE TEST OF INFANCY YOUVE CLUNG TO IS ONLY ITS BEGINNING. CALL ME.

Dad died five years late. Long after making what the doctors called a "Hollywood recovery," on a morning when the ground's ice was young and invisible, he fell and broke his head open on a right-angle of the concrete stair just outside his front door. He bled into membranes beneath his skull until they bloated and gently suffocated his brain. No one noticed him lying there until the following morning.

IT WAS 13 HOURS, 45 MINUTES ON 07
THE 2ND AND SUCH AS IT WAS THE
57TH HOUR, 49TH MINUTES THAT THE
DEPOSIT WAS DISCOVERED. NONE
ELSE MADE USE OF THIS SPEECH.
BECOME AS IMPORTANT AS YOUR LIFE.
WATCH + DISCOVER A NEW WAY. BUT
KNOW ALWAYS OUR ATTENTION
ATTRACTS FEAR.

He outlived his wife by three years and change, which should probably be worth something but didn't feel like it. Mid-way through her husband's chemo, she learned of her own small, insistent tumors woven-in deep throughout her body. She hated the thought of being a bother, so she didn't make a peep, and one day her husband woke up and the woman by his side just simply wasn't there anymore.

THE THIRD RING OF THE HAMMER
BEING ALL JUST AND PERFECT,
DECLARES THE BEGINNING OF AUGUST
RESPECTFUL AND SYMBOLIC RITUAL OF
SILENCE.

/1404er/ didn't attend her funeral. (He hadn't seen her since the aborted dinner handsy weirdness. Things were different after that.) It was the last he and his father spoke, though later on they'd exchange small e-mails, maybe every three or four months, and dad still made sure his son had something to eat; dry microwave rations by his door on the weekly.

SEEK THE TRUTH? SHE IS ON HER
FACE. SEEK THE FEAR THEN ACCEPT
DEATH OF THOSE IF NOT YOURSELF.
OR IF, YOUR FACE PRESENTS A SMILE?

LET IT BE FREE. AS PRESENTS THE HIDDEN, SO AS TO BE TRUE.

He also skipped dad's funeral. It'd been almost six years since he'd been outside his room at all.

TO SEE DEATH WILL BE TO SEE THE TRUTH, THE DAWN SILENCE HOUSE FILLS THE UNHAPPY SOUL. DARKNESS COMES ALIVE THEN WHEN WE CAN SEE OUR FEARS IN THE LIGHT. THE FOOD BAD? DOES THOU NEED THE EVIL OF LIGHT TO TORMENT YOUR NIGHTS?

Maybe he was gone. Maybe he was still there.

THEN SLOWLY OPEN YOUR EYES OUT OF DEEPEST LONELINESS. FULFILL WHAT WILL BE ASKED. BUT BE CAREFUL WITH THE WAY YOU TREAT WITH US. WHAT IS THE NAME BY WHICH WE TAKE SOMETHING? FOR NOW WE WILL TAKE ALL WHO LOVE HIM, AND THEY WILL REALIZE HIS NAME IS A CURSE. CALL ME.

WATCH: http://0nlowestcomm61.onion |
http://pros972_0.onion |
http://play10772firstvvvvp.onion |
http://jz65play00tears.onion |
http://48mq7taken.onion |
http://payed_9893_2drain933.onion |
http://nsj87krool99ty.onion |
http://2o76_big730_forest89210.onion |

http://open111_03682ashtrey.onion |
http://pl7n398ca7ean.onion

There were things about them he missed. He missed how they used to give him things, and how his mom would actually cook the meals she delivered. He missed how they brought him the packages he ordered, usually without question. All erased now.

►Public Grief Fuck
►/1404er/ (Tue) 17:30:19 No.30857028394
hey, so these total pieces of hunan garbage just lost their kid, and instead of doing the normal thing they're doing a jewgle hangout pity party. way to live it up, dongalongs. let'em know what you think.

https://plus.google.com/hangouts/_/wtl/sXLC rn0Q_2Xvus3bCvugL27Rs4cdZuQIRIbDuU9 swew=?hl=en_US&authuser=0

And there names are Tyler and Irene Olana, if you can find anything else on them. i guess the kid drowned or something.

But they left /1404er/ in good standing. Dad didn't sabotage his inheritance. (Blood can make you do a lot of things.) He got the house—fully paid for—and the $760,103 nest egg, plus the $116,040 in assets. He could quit his job with the knowledge his life wouldn't have to change in any significant manner. Everything had worked out. Except for what he was going to eat.

►/1404er/ (Tue) 17:37:19 No.30857028427
f.b. memorial:
facebook.com/loved_qz0tiffany_jeffrey

►/1404er/ (Tue) 17:39:41 No.30857028433
kid is getting so much dicks on his page

►/1404er/ (Tue) 17:41:01 No.30857028440
drowned n dicks

He managed a day and a half without eating, after his stockpile of instant kung pao ran out. He halfway convinced himself he could compel his body to mutate—to subsist on materials devoid of properties like fats, sugars, cholesterol and calcium. He stuffed his mouth with dry paper. He stuffed his mouth with his hair. His stomach's walls twisted and swarmed with acid and threatened ulcer.

►/1404er/ (Tue) 17:49:55 No.30857028501
link is dead whats going on

►/1404er/ (Tue) 17:52:43 No.30857028517
>>>30857028501
they shut it down pretty quick and ar prob hugboxxxin it out rn but it was some pretty entertaning autism while it lasted

He found a nearby pizza place with help from the Computer. The Computer still wanted him alive. The Computer found his address and the name of his city. It'd been years since /1404er/ had considered his geography. The Computer's internal GPS sent words and numbers to the Computer's face, and told him he lived at 3599 Nordstrom Lane, Windsor Locks, Connecticut. 06096.

►/1404er/ (Tue) 17:54:59 No.30857028522
shit. been too long since i spit on a grave.
was amped for this.

He placed the order through the website, without having to talk to anyone, and tension released from his form.

He'd never have to leave. Mom and dad could just be gone. He felt okay about that. He liked the way pizza tastes. But he couldn't keep from weeping because he knew he'd have to go into the hall and down the stairs and see a person.

►/1404er/ (Tue) 18:03:11 No.30857028613
got another f.b. memorial, looks untouched.
kid was 6 and had fucking bone cancer. talk
about fucked since birth
merry xmas:
facebook.com/98vT_love_is_a_monument

He was certain he was going to fall. The stairs were odd and alien. It'd been so long. But he made it down, step by step, paw-over-paw tied to the rail. The odor took him back a decade. His parents still hanging in the air. His father's collections of dust.

Everyone has their dust; unique in arrangement and composition. His mother's was far more subtle and integrated into her surroundings, therefore quickly usurped in the years since she passed. /1404er/ couldn't find a trace of her. His father never cleaned more than what was necessary to keep appearances, and his dust gathered in regions obscured by furniture and shadow.

He couldn't remember his father's face and character, but he remembered his dust. He saw it everywhere in the downstairs. Mite-nests of coiled grey hair atop glazes of skin cells.

▶/1404er/ (Tue) 18:05:05 No.30857028620
jesus christ are you guys the whateverth
level of hell?

His dad had splurged on a nice 65" curved-face flatscreen during his last year. Television didn't interest /1404er/ at all. TV was just a computer but stupid.

▶/1404er/ (Tue) 18:07:46 No.30857028629
gtfo

A lifetime ago, when his parent's were alive and he still moved about the house, /1404er/ could always stomach his father's dust. It never irritated his throat or caused his sinus to clog with viscous slugs and other methods of defense. His body remained immune to its affects, even after so many years of sustained absence.

He sat on the couch, and waited for the doorbell to ring. He worried the delivery person would want to say words and he worried he'd have to say words back. He couldn't remember what his voice sounded like, and he was too scared to practice.

▶/1404er/ (Tue) 18:10:31 No.30857028640
faggot, we don't do this for the sake of the
departed. we do this for those they leave
behind. just like any memorial.

He didn't need to speak, or even touch the man's fingers. It wasn't even a man—a boy, three years his junior, but with a presence that felt decades older. He just handed over the big brown box, turned around and walked away.

It worked. /1404er/ could stay inside forever.

*   *   *

XIII

►The Esoteric (.onion dump)
►/1404er/ (Sun) 16:00:18 No.30857914973
Dump the difficult stuff. The stuff you don't
understand entirely.
Intel Exchange:
http://wrbb9zqpyuv3xe9p.onion/
New Coastlines:
http://vnn912tuyvnqgua.onion/
Buried Secrets:
http://answers792heartbeak.onion/
The Left Circle:
http://valumtide.741z9v.onion/
and of course the fun and suprising and
usually horrifying random.prize.onion

/1404er/ got used to spending time downstairs, with his
parents gone. Novelty was frightening but could be nice when
he got used to it. Being downstairs taught him how to stare at
a wall again.

►/1404er/ (Sun) 16:06:06 No.30857915009
http://valp8.origns.onion.link/ - Keys Open
Doors
http://cazz3docks04.onion.link/ - Day Life
Generator
http://d4v-crat7crat.onion.link/ - Rusky Shit

http://vir39blckwethr.onion.link/ - Wyrm Hold
http://rifterkin44vy4.onion.link/ - New Dark
Rites

►/1404er/ (Sun) 16:08:37 No.30857915018
Orchid Grind- http://blau01vjsherst.onion/

►/1404er/ (Sun) 16:09:04 No.30857915019
No CP I presume?

►/1404er/ (Sun) 16:11:58 No.30857915030
>>>30857915019
no, unless related

When he was little and in bed with his mother's sleep, he'd
focus all his attention to the bumps and inconsistencies of her
bedside wall. Pure minutia. He would trace the small cracks
and stipling with his retina, bringing him to the edge of null
state, until his mother would turn and brush her body against
his side, and he'd fall backwards from oblivion and scraped
Zen.

►/1404er/ (Sun) 16:15:02 No.30857915048
occult & numbers
http://gull4bq7yard.onion/weblog/index.html

►/1404er/ (Sun) 16:18:29 No.30857915061
http://30y7crawl.thru.onion/–# Grey Crawl
http://cr0maloy4.00.onion/ –# Scroll All
http://1067dyrtnp.onion/ –# Burier
http://blessed.zeram.onion.link/ –# Zeram
Worship
http://75no9weight.onion.link/refs/ –# Game
Theory

He only ever used a fraction of the house. Mostly the living room, and his bedroom, still. The kitchen made him nervous. He didn't want to go in there. His mother's place. Sometimes he used the downstairs and upstairs hallway bathrooms, as a change of scenery, almost. Never set foot in mom and dad's room. His old room. A lifetime ago.

Decades later, after /1404er/'s own passing, men and women from the state will find his parents' belongings sealed away in that bedroom, just as his father had left them. It will be seized and auctioned off and, given age, lose all semblance of relevance and dissolve and be lost.

►/1404er/ (Sun) 16:27:45 No.30857915103
http://5vgy7poisonoak.onion/ - Anarchy Directory
http://14fortified.onion/ - The Armory (not what you think)
http://6r4xcvv8mtr.onion/ - Gee, I wonder what the fuck this is?
http://7ialader98qp0t.onion/ - General Blasphemy
http://differ.712muffns.onion/ - Abomination
http://tvy0drag.me.onion/ - The Insides

He got back into staring at walls by watching light move. Light had always captivated him. How the road's high beams slivered through the blinds and raked across the walls and his body. Or the silent orange and pink hum stamped to window shades in the sun's recession. Before, it had been dominated by the Computer's face. Now he'd put his face in whatever light he found and close his eyes, becoming throbbing salmon and peach. He'd open and let the buzz fade, and return to the wall, inspecting its cracks and bumps until he began to disappear. A doze and a half-dream of empty swaths and shifting forms over void, infinite and indefinable.

▶/1404er/ (Sun) 16:32:23 No.30857915135
http://carcin0919.onion/ - Paralyzer
http://zv3nettle.onion/imageboard/ -
NettleChan
http://allhisspunk.onion/sites.html - Links by
Harris (has interesting... stuff)
http://uy88caver.onion/ - How Will You Tell
The World?

▶/1404er/ (Sun) 16:33:18 No.30857915137
http://xuq9lue1hori70n.onion/index.php –
Code of Conquest

▶/1404er/ (Sun) 16:35:47 No.30857915151
Patient Zero -
http://zeroeramust5deltacldxvy.onion/

And eventually he'd wake, stiff up on his parent's couch.
Alone in the stretching night. He'd wipe his eyes and climb the
stairs back to his bedroom, and collapse amidst the crusted up
sweats atop the mattress. He'd sleep, again. It didn't matter so
much anymore whether the Computer was turned off all the
way, and he barely touched his dick at all.

▶/1404er/ (Sun) 16:40:12 No.30857915172
I just bumped into some monarch-tier shit
using random.prize. I need to stop coming
here

▶/1404er/ (Sun) 16:41:39 No.30857915175
http://72trunufate.onion/ - the world in the
back of my head

* * *

XIV

The downstairs provided atmosphere for other things to grow. He walked among saplings, watering them with his body's moisture and heat. New inertia and subroutines; whole frontiers of blank. Ghosts emerging from his insides.

When he was little he could sit by his mother's and father's skin without nausea, and the three would crowd the couch and watch light across the TV's face. All their bodies together and the news always on. He hated the news anchors. So frightening. Plastic skin but before the age he fell for plastic skin.

The ghosts made his hands quiver. They let him close the boards and turn the Computer off all the way. They kept him in the downstairs and aimed his face at its walls. They pushed him toward the kitchen, until he'd cover his ears and squeeze his eyes tight and wheeze *no.*

The anchor's voice was plastic string and forks in surge sockets, interrogating a woman in her twenties. Her face glazed and happy and flush under light. Ankles unseen, half-embedded in dirt.

The sun began its dip behind the horizon and the walls sunk to augmented beige, and he could feel his body in the walls forty years later. Stuck inside, spasming and mostly not breathing.

He opened his eyes and saw the wall as spilled and spread viscera, ripe to divine. The ghosts looked out from his body, translating the organs he dreamed.

The big story was she had given her future away. She was letting her body become destroyed. And she was so happy. They went and shot her for her last three days and all the time she was so happy.

Sometimes he felt inside his father's face and body; residuals drifted through from months or years long past. His father's wanderings and subroutines. The couch. The bathroom. The kitchen (the most frightening place). An office. The space where his father abandoned them for hours and half-days. He knew it existed but couldn't remember where. He didn't want to ever go through the entire house, but the ghosts said he'd have to.

"When I read about Gerry, I immediately—I just knew that he was the person I was put here for." She was laughing and crying, but her smile and eyes were bigger than choking out of air. She knew the day after next she wouldn't be alive anymore, so all of time stretched forward and became ecstatic and beautiful. Cut to a hospital, and a bed, and the man who was taking her heart away.

He didn't know the ghosts. Just that they came from inside him. At first he thought they were his mom and dad of course but that wasn't true. They were more than just one or two, or a measurable number, or a name you could give to something. They stood higher than time but not of inverse composition; valleys in his brain yanked down and spanning decades. Ghosts always hanging somewhere near. He listened to them speak and it felt like a lung collapse. They told him things about his father. They told him he should kill himself. He'd slap his cheeks and stab the couch with his fists until they relented.

"I always wanted a shot of just me—just me walking through the surf at night." The moon was new and amplified over oil-black Atlantic. Her clothes soaked and skin goose-fleshed and shivered. Her face didn't show; just wide open agape at the dusk. The boom bobbing in and out of shot. Her arms twined around her ribcage. Crying with a smile on. "It's like a movie. Isn't it? Isn't it just like it?"

They knew everything about him. Broaching memories he couldn't even recall. Every thread and post. Every frame that had stilled his insides. Every impetus and means.

They shot her with her family, and with the man taking her life. His eyes sorrowed and engulfed. A creature who could never live forever, no matter the age of the heart stuffed in his body.

The ghosts needled at his spine. Probing for his father's space, with sharp spider nails and teeth. When he'd resist they'd make him hurt. They ran their fingers up and down his intestines until he queased and sprung ulcers. They kneaded his brain into seizure. They bloated him with aches and fever, prying flesh and extremity toward the kitchen, where his mother had lived. For hours or days. Trembling his ribcage and scraping his prostate. They wanted to show him things. And when squeezing his skull and beating the couch cushions no longer exhausted them, he pulled onto his feet, and drifted atop the hardwood toward the kitchen's doorframe.

They shot the operation, blurring some gore but not all. She didn't look like a person anymore, and eventually, off-camera, they let her stop breathing. He clutched his tiny hands around the bare substance of his body. He imagined what it felt like to give your insides away.

The kitchen had knives and fire, but they didn't frighten him like he thought they would. His being in there didn't alter his biology or chromosomes or sense of being. Calm and quiet, like the other rooms. The ghosts stopped scraping, and knots unwound from his back. He let himself feel stupid for his fear and faithless mind. An unfamiliar door stood across the room, and the ghosts whispered him toward its handle.

"Do you think she did the right thing?" The anchor's voice dead and composed. "I *know* she did the right thing." Her father sobbed. "She did the right thing. But none of that means I have to be happy with it." His face red with buried blood and fluorescent heat. "So much." Blubber after blubber. "It hurts so much."

Cut to his daughter walking through the surf, weeks passed, salt glazed across her smile knowing that in days she would become only the most basic and central aspect of herself. The part that throbbed solely of mass and energy, divorced from any discernible thought or sensation.

* * *

XV

Notice: ###### ROOM RULES ######

Notice: Rule #1: *I* run the show, not you.

Notice: Rule #2: Tip for request *only*

Notice: Rule #3: ENGLISH ONLY

Notice: Rule #4: no "bb"

ChachiBoi has joined Hvn_Snt-8686's room

massageboz: there not 2 big im not worried about it

Hvn_Snt-8686: *omgod chachi!!!! :* :**

massageboz: neway...

Hvn_Snt-8686: *where have u been?!?!?!*

Hvn_Snt-8686: *i missed u!!!!!!!*

massageboz tipped 50 tokens

109

The office was his father's dust. Dead cells and follicles, and his papers and books. His furniture. His pens and calculator. His pill bottles. His laptop. It all could have been his ashes.

The ghosts stayed quiet in there. They didn't need to tell him not to touch anything. Not to touch anything but the laptop. So he slowly pulled open his father's Computer's face. It lit up suddenly, independent of any further action. It had been sleeping. So long. Now it was awake.

HENRY stands over the bathroom sink in the night, hands wrapped around a drinking glass. His body shakes. Press CONTROL as fast as you can to maintain HENRY's grip, and ALT to fill the glass with water. If you fail, HENRY will drop it and get shards in his feet.

►/anonymous/ 06.24.2024 15:47:00 No.10086946
You don't pick your parents, you don't pick your genes, you don't pick the environment in which those genes were expressed, you don't assemble the micro and macro structures of your brain which decide every conscious and unconscious action you will make in your 2.5 billion seconds of life, you don't choose the thoughts in which you think. What makes you think you have any free will whatsoever.

►/anonymous/ 06.24.2024 15:53:29 No.10086951
they are brought to my counciousness by my

subconciousness and both are produced by my brain, so it'd be correct to consider them my own thoughts.

▶/anonymous/   06.24.2024
15:55:09 No.10086957
Yes but that is not "free" will, that is simply witnessing choices being made by your subconscious.

▶/anonymous/   06.24.2024
15:57:43 No.10086965
who is witnessing this stuff? I'm saying I'm both my concious and my subconcious.

▶/anonymous/   06.24.2024
16:00:01 No.10086971
Your conscious mind, seeing how you can't witness your subconscious mind.

▶/anonymous/   06.24.2024
16:02:51 No.10086978
so I'm witnessing myself

Across its face was a window, and the window lead to the entire world and everything in it. A window that had been his father's eyes and nuance. Part of his story still stuck in there. And from it, part of a ghost crawled from the laptop's husk and pressed through /1404er/'s pores. It guided his hand to a grey death track pad and ivory keys. The ghosts steadied his eyes and translated his father's language.

SUPPORT EMU-ENDO
register now!

CHOOSE A ROM
abracablaster.rom
cannonboss.rom
circlesdrain.rom
cowboyburial.rom
dazzlersofeurekamore.rom
demoncough.rom
denihilfight.rom

{LOAD}
OPTIONS
KEYBOARD SETUP
GRAPHICS
SOUND

NEW GAME and START and dissolve to black and a small man emerging, and letters forming words and exposition.

NAME: HENRY KOWJOLSKI
AGE: 87
OCCUPATION: FARMER
HENRY HAS BEEN REAL FORGETFUL LATELY, SO SOMETIMES HE NEEDS A HELPING HAND WITH CHORES AROUND THE FARM. HELP HIM KEEP THE PACE!

Notice: ##### ROOM RULES ######
Notice: Rule #1: no bb
Notice: Rule #2: tip for requests
Notice: Rule #3: be polite
Notice: Rule #4: no politics

ChachiBoi has joined Ju_cKarla6's room

Ju cKarla6: *chachiboi!!!!!!!!!!!*
b1tch1nsp3ctr: feet plz

Ju_cKarla6 has sent you a private message
Ju cKarla6: *hey bb u wan privt?*
Ju cKarla6: *tell me where to put it*

Directory> Folder> vids & plix>
>anniversary14.mov
>bj1.mov
>bj2.mov
>blackgarters.jpg
>bluteddy.jpg
>cation(holland).mov
>redress.jpg
>test3.mov
>usboth2.mov
>vday16.mov
>washington.mov

NAME: ALANA KOWJOLSKI
AGE: 84
OCCUPATION: HENRY'S WIFE
ALANA HAS BEEN REAL TIRED AND QUIET LATELY. LET'S SEE IF THERE'S SOMETHING WE CAN DO TO HELP!

Directory>Safari>Bookmarks>
>/tech/

>helpdesk.org
>Rom-Central
>/sci/
>Game Palace
>House of Mind: When
Children Withdraw
>Did Alzheimer's Rates
Really Go Up in 201...
>https://www.youtube.com/
watch?v=Z8-dl...
>ChildDev.org: Anti-Social
Personality Disor...
>Teen Killer: "I masturbate
to your tear-filled...
>WebMD: Symptom
Search
>Why Are 700,00
Japanese Men Locking...
...

In all the pictures and videos of his mother, her skin looked as plastic as he'd wanted but her breasts so different from his dreams. Something like deformity. Sometimes he saw his father too, but only his body. His cock like wet cardboard.

Gold sunbeams fall through windows and fill the room with light. Gravity lifted with birdcalls and dog barks. HENRY yawns and stretches arms over head.

> *HENRY: GOOD MORNING, ALANA.*
> *ALANA: GOOD MORNING, DEAR.*
> *HENRY: ANOTHER BEAUTIFUL DAY OUT, TODAY.*
> *ALANA: THAT'S NICE, DEAR.*

114

HENRY says THERE'S DUST ON EVERYTHING! ALANA says I'M SO TIRED. Push HENRY out the bedroom through the door to the SOUTH. Push HENRY down the stairs to the kitchen. Make him look in the refrigerator and EAT MOLDY CASSEROLE, EAT OLD STEAK or DRINK EXPIRED MILK, or do nothing at all. Eating or drinking will have no effect on the game. Exit to the porch through the door to the WEST.

►/anonymous/   06.24.2024
16:07:11 No.10086999
Free will is the ability to choose between different possible courses of action.

Cognition is the set of all mental abilities and processes related to knowledge, attention, memory and working memory, judgment and evaluation, reasoning and computation, problem solving and decision making, comprehension and production of language, etc

Thus free will exists and is proportional to cognition. The lower the cognition, the less guilty you are. Fun fact: anti-social people like to think of themselves as smart asses, therefore they are even more guilty than average if their intelligence exceptional.

Notice: ###### ROOM RULES ######
Notice: Rule #1: tip the performer
Notice: Rule #2: no demands, no bbs
Notice: Rule #3: 500 c2c
Notice: Rule #4: privates on

ChachiBoi has joined Melanie-Model's room

puzyplzr: talk about the last guy that fucked you
Sp3rmyM1ke: u do anal?
Melanie-Model: *privates live, 22 token/min*

puzyplzr was silenced and his comments were removed from the chat log

Melanie-Model has sent you a private message
Melanie-Model: *mmm where have u bin?*
Melanie-Model: *I was missin u*

Alternate between pressing the keys assigned to the CTRL and ALT buttons to milk the cow's teats. Alternate between pressing CTRL and ALT until the timer runs out. When the timer runs out, HENRY looks at the bucket and says I TUGGED AS HARD AS I COULD, BUT NO MILK CAME OUT! It doesn't matter which cow you milk or how many times you press CTRL and ALT, this is the only possible outcome.

Push HENRY into the garden through the gate to the WEST. Press CTRL to make him try and pull up the vegetables. HENRY says either NOTHING'S GROWING or LOOKS LIKE THE GOPHER GOT IN AGAIN. You cannot harvest any vegetables.

Walk HENRY SOUTH to the chicken coops and stand him next to the grain barrel. Press CTRL to make him pick up a handful of grain. Stand him next to the chicken coops and press CTRL to feed the chickens. HENRY says THERE AREN'T ANY CHICKENS TO FEED....

There is nothing else to do here, so push HENRY back into the house.

Directory>Safari>Bookmarks>

...

>NDL
>hidden-wiki.onion
>/philosophy/
>Apocalypse Now: 5 Ways the World Could...
>The Internet's New Radical Right
>Cancer Connection
>/1404er/: We don't argue with those we di...
>Did Alzheimer's Rates Really Increase Thi...
>NatGeo: The Reality of Black Holes

...

it's not like we are trapped in our
bodies, we are our bodies, so the
result of our thought processes is
our free will. It's not free from the
laws of nature, but then nothing
is, so it's pointless to expect
somethign else.

You expect some kind of
divine/transcendent qualities for
free will, but that isn't a necessity
at all.

*See the small flashing dot on the sink. Stand HENRY in front
of it and press CTRL. HENRY says I THINK ALANA SAID I
NEED TO TAKE THESE PILLS. Make him take the pills or
don't. Your choice will have no effect on the game.*

*Push HENRY up the stairs and back into the bedroom.
The day has passed and ALANA is still in bed. Make HENRY
try to talk to her. Henry says SHE'S NOT BREATHING.*

SHE'S NOT BREATHING.
SHE'S NOT BREATHING.
SHE'S NOT BREATHING.
SHE'S NOT BREATHING.
SHE'S NOT BREATHING.
SHE'S NOT BREATHING.
SHE'S NOT BREATHING.

**Notice: ###### ROOM RULES
######
Notice: Rule #1: BE NICE
Notice: Rule #2: NO
PRIVATES/C2C**

118

Notice: Rule #3: NO DEMANDS
Notice: Rule #4: NO BB
*ChachiBoi has joined
GODdessRey88's room*

puzyplzr: talk about the last guy
that fucked you

*GODdessRey88 has sent you a
private message*

*There is a man in a business suit and a woman dressed in
white standing in HENRY's kitchen. Make him talk to the man.
He says I THINK...THIS IS MY SON? Press CTRL again, he
says WHY IS HE SAYING HE'S SORRY? CTRL again, and
HE SAYS HE'LL TAKE CARE OF EVERYTHING?*

*Make him talk to the woman. HENRY says I CAN'T
UNDERSTAND WHAT SHE'S SAYING. Press CTRL again,
he says I DON'T LIKE WHAT SHE'S SAYING. CTRL again,
and he says WHAT DOES SHE MEAN?*

*Walk him EAST to the dining room and NORTH to the
bathroom. Set him in front of the mirror and make him say I
DON'T EVEN RECOGNIZE MYSELF ANYMORE.*

Directory>Safari>Bookmarks>
...
>Connecticut
Craigslist>Personals>Casual
>right here right
now (can host)-wfm
>grad looking for
older cock-wfm
>need to pay
student loans-wfm

>nsa cutie in need
of a rubdown-wfm
>MindHQ.com: This is
Your Brain On Grief
>24 Hour Bereavement
Chat
>The Widower's Resource
>camdivas.us:
>candy_Ellis
>SweetPeech
>Melanie-Model
>trinity_luvs
>Kassie-sweatZ
>/grief/

ChachiBoi has joined Kassie-sweatZ's room

Kassie-sweatZ:hi chachiboi!!!!!

It's a pack of mangy wild dogs howling and pawing the side of the barn. They hiss and cackle when HENRY wobbles toward them. Press ALT and bring up the shotgun's crosshairs. Use the arrow keys to line up the crosshair. Press CTRL and HENRY shoots. The dogs turn to wet and red. Killing the dogs has no effect on the game.

The performers' faces scrunched weird; /1404er/ speaking through his father's keys. The performers ask *what's wrong*. He closes out the window and touches his dick but it feels like it belongs to someone else.

of course we don't have any free will. free will doesn't exist, just like computers don't exist. all things are arrangements of atoms. people classify and define nouns according to their functions: tables are arrangements of atoms, emotions are terms for results of arrangements of atoms that dictate further rearrangements of atoms, etc blah blah.

free will is a useful abstraction for expressing constraints, such as conscientiousness, something OP is incapable of expressing and which he therefore believes does not exist.

"but words don't exist, only sounds do!"

OP fuck off. humans don't think in terms of reality. we build models.

Please take this shit to reddit.

HENRY lays in darkness. The floors, walls and furniture cast blue and cinder, and some hum outside. His body shakes. He can't keep from crying and he's not quite sure why. Push him

out of bed, and his room, and down the stairs into the kitchen
and out the door.

Outside is a blurred unearthly dark. Purple mist hanging
off the oxygen. Chunks of ground scooped from this dimension
and swapped with negative space.

Push HENRY to the barn collapsed to rot and splinter.
Push him WEST to the garden swollen with flies. Push him
SOUTH to the chicken coops blown asunder among animal
bone. Or push him back inside. Nothing you do will have any
effect on the game.

Make him accept that there was nothing he could do to
keep his loved ones safe forever. Make him accept that there
was never any way to replace the bits of self that gradually
fell away. Make him accept that he will come out of this world
as nothing more than matter and electricity, and in time no
one will know he was ever here to begin with. Press CTRL to
close his eyes. Release to make him let go.

It was weird and short and kind of pointless, and mostly he
didn't like the way it made his stomach feel. He shut off the
Computer and pulled out its plug.

A bell chimes. HENRY's world twists into fractals and dancing
golden hoops. Men and women without faces flicker as
particles; their only lasting evidence. No thought or language.
Slow dissolve. There is nothing else to do. There are no other
endings.

He hit the laptop with a hardbound IT manual he found on one
of the shelves, cracking the Computer's enamel. He did some
other things, then walked upstairs and went to bed.

Too clear for memory; hues too bold and indelible to belong
to anything physical. But he knows he was here long ago when
he was small, outside with them, outside in the clear wet and

bright gold shine over red yellow blue, the plastics and rubbers. The wave pool and leviathan hollow crab he climbed up inside and throughout, firing its spigots at all living children.

There's a crowd encircled in the deepest wet of circular color, and he as a child reaches his eyes over everyone's shoulders to spot who has drowned, but his mother and father are just as massive as their grins and they blot him like moons between Earth and sun.

His eyes crack and bleed and go blurry and the wet tastes like leaked garbage, and though he can hardly see he can feel his father's identifying calluses along his belly and cock, and then familiar lips and teeth. (Are they really familiar?) And his mother smiling through her tears, but only the smile is real and the tears this time are pretend. Something he dreamed but had never immersed. And he remembers the lie he told himself, when he first learned how to twist his world's dynamics. That he could bend synapse with noises through his mouth from his lobes, and later through his fingers. Stitching up what they or anyone could fear. Orange as a candle with all night surrounding it, and dead fish and dogs. Feeling real snuffed so quiet, so clear. Too clear to be any kind of memory.

He woke to cold semen wads half-crusted inside his sweatpants. He got up, turned on the Computer (his Computer) and ordered a pizza through its face. Then he drowned the ghosts in the downstairs bathtub and blew six thousand dollars on a RealDoll.

* * *

XVI

▶ i think i killed a bitch
▶ /1404er/ (Mon) 23:13:11 No.3085900329
saw a girl on f.b i used to high school with.
sent her a message from a fake account.
told her i knew her from school and that i had
nudes of her, and that i'd send them to her
family if she didn't film herself doing some
stuff for me. total shot in the dark, i had
nothing. she believed me though.

It arrived in a wooden crate. A sarcophagus. He didn't like
how the deliverymen had to come inside, but there wasn't any
other way. /1404er/ didn't say words to them, but grunted and
pointed instruction with his fingers.

"'kay, sign here." Taking the pen from the man's hand felt
disgusting. "You got something to open this, right?" He was
much taller than /1404er/ but his words disguised fear.
/1404er/ swung his head side to side and shrugged; knives
coming out of his face.

The other deliveryman (or maybe a woman, or both or
neither. He couldn't tell anymore) unlatched a crowbar from
his belt and handed it to the filthy, trembling boy. "On the
house, bruh. We've got plenty of these."

They left, laughing timid, and /1404er/ was alone with his
box and the future.

►/1404er/ (Mon) 23:14:59 No.3085900331
spent months making her do all kinds of sick
shit (rubbing piss on her face, fucking her
asshole with a plunger, pussy with a
cucumber, punch herself hard in the face).
learned the best thing to do was go easy
every once in a while, but I pushed too hard
one day. she snapped and went on f.b and
makes this long dramatic ass post. tells her
friends, coworkers, and family about
everything I've been making her do. posts
screenshots of our texts and my contact info.
says she's going to kill herself. that she
knows god wont mind accepting another
angle into his kingdom. like 40 people in the
comments begging her not to. 20 mins later
it's taken down. never heard from her again.
can't find her on social media. few days later
everyone's sharing her obit on f.b.

The crate broke apart with more ease than expected and a
body collapsed from white and orange peanuts. Wrapped in
textile; ones people would maybe wear. Its waist twisted on
the floor face down and arms sprawled like a fall down stairs.
A sliver of vagina peaked from red underwear and a miniskirt.

**►/1404er/ (Mon) 23:16:03
No.3085900333**
it's been a while so i think i'm in
the clear. i was pretty slick about
how i went about it.
Pic: pssyitch.jpg (2 MB)
(her pouring piss on her face)

http://blasphbq.12v9trash-immac8v.onion/
TRASHED IMMACULANCE
DONATE/UPLOAD

SUBMIT USING MYBOX OR MEGLO.
(DO **NOT** SEND VIDEO AS AN ATTACHEMENT!!!!!!) THEN SEND THE LINK TO MY EMAIL: Q28ox733kQikZAlLwnBQxly5@maestromessage.ch

►/1404er/ (Mon) 23:20:34
No.3085900347
Alright edgelord if you're so psychotic,tell everyone here your name and address and go to your closest neighbors. Kill them and carve "for the glory of /1404er/s" on their backs. You won't because you're a dick head child on Xmas break lying about shit on the Internet.

►/1404er/ (Mon) 23:21:41
No.3085900348
Not that I believe your bullshit story anyway, but if someone was worried about vanilla nudes getting out from high school (not even mentioning the fact that it would most likely be child porn and the fact that you "had" them would put you in greater risk than

anybody), why would you trust
that person with recordings of
you doing totally depraved shit
like rubbing piss on your face?

The factory named it Ce Ce, but he didn't want it to have a
name. He didn't want it to be a person. Just a body and a
thing, with skin like rubber. That wouldn't cry or yield from
abuse. Possess desires or dreams of its own, or talk back or
even say words at all. He didn't want the doll to have a name.

►/1404er/ (Mon) 23:24:23
No.3085900361
because she was an idiot. and
she had a pretty fucked up life.
she finally got her shit together
and got a job and a bf who she
claimed was the love of her life. i
guess she didn't wanna lose that.
heres   some   more   proof:
http://meglo.ic/9b73zq19

►/1404er/ (Mon) 23:31:49
No.3085900387
Ok I believe you now.

Why would you do something like
that? I'm not sitting in judgment
but I was a corrections counselor
for years and I just kind of want
to know what motivated you to do
something like this.

RENAME YOUR VIDEO FILE SOMETHING RANDOM LIKE 'VACATION' OR 'GRADUATION'

**►/1404er/ (Mon) 23:33:52
No.3085900394**
well i didn't think it was going to work. and when it did, it felt great. when you're in a normal relationship, no matter how kinky your girl is, there's always compromise. i just wanted to see what it felt like to not have to deal with that.and it felt good but wrong. i'd be lying if said i didn't feel real guilty afterwards.

**►/1404er/ (Mon) 23:37:12
No.3085900405**
u still hav the plunger vid?

He just let it lay there a long while. He stared at it as if it were a wall; tracing its curves and contours without touching. He touched his dick but it was soft. He thought about food going cold and wet time and tile and a dent knocked deep in a bathroom wall.

**►/1404er/ (Mon) 23:41:50
No.3085900422**
the fucked up thing is i don't have 90% of what she filmed. she used dropbox to share the vids, since they were too big to email and she wasn't ok with a host site. but i didn't know dropbox

had a very limited gb capacity, so everytime she sent one, she also deleted one.

tl;dr: don't have that one

RULES
►-MUST BE GOOD QUALITY (NOT BLURRED OUT)
►-CAN NOT BE FOUND ON OTHER SITES
►-ONLY VIDEOS WITH THE FACE VISIBLE WILL BE ACCEPTED
►-WE PREFER YOUR OWN HOMEMADE MATERIAL (IF YOU HAVE SOME MATERIAL WHERE YOU ARE ALSO ON IT, AND YOU WANT YOURSELF OUT OF THE VIDEO, SEND THE ORIGINAL, WE EDIT IT HOW YOU WANT IT AND PUT IT BACK UP).

►/1404er/ (Mon) 23:50:28
No.3085900493
If I could ask you...
How old are you?
What is your general opinion regarding women?
Do you have many successful relationships?
Would others consider you well adjusted?
Do you have a history of mental health problems - diagnosed or undiagnosed?
Do you hold a job? Can I ask what you do?
Were you cruel to animals as a child?

It took hours to even approach it. Like at any moment it could have woken up. He imagined its fingers around his neck and stuffed down his mouth. He pictured it biting through his bones and sinew. But he kept his approach and reached out to touch the body.

PLEASE, DO NOT SEND VIDEOS WITH DEAD STUFF, FAKE, AMATEUR, MASTURBATION OR ACTED SCENES.
IF THE VIDEO IS NEW TO US AND FOLLOWS THE RULES, YOU WILL RECEIVE EXCLUSIVE VIDS FROM MY PERSONAL COLLECTION.

▶/1404er/ (Mon) 24:01:43
No.3085900554
didn't expect this to be an AMA
>>>*How old are you?*
in my 20's
>>>*What is your general opinion regarding women?*
some are good some are bad. but it hurts more when they're bad because they're supposed to be the good ones.
>>>*Do you have many successful relationships?*
never been in a relationship for more than a year.
>>>*Do you have a history of mental health problems - diagnosed or undiagnosed?*

Would others consider you well adjusted?
well adjusted? i have a thing about crowds but i haven't been diagnosed with anything.
>>>Do you hold a job? Can I ask what you do?
currently unemployed but i've worked various jobs since i was young. mostly tech retail and IT
>>>Were you cruel to animals as a child?
i used to hit this dog i used to have but i stopped. i'm honestly very ashamed about that. it was a good dog.

►/1404er/ (Mon) 24:01:47
No.3085900555
How about the cucumer vid?

Its hair felt too much like hair. Its mouth felt too much like a mouth. Its breasts felt too much like his mother's breast. Its eyes shifted and rattled in an empty skull, and looked so, so scared.

►/1404er/ (Mon) 24:04:32
No.3085900572
no cucumber. what I posted is what i've got.

►/1404er/ (Mon) 24:07:05
No.3085900592
You're a very interesting case. Have you considered talking to a

psychologist? You don't have to tell them about anything you did regarding the girl, but you might find that it's helpful to have a safe place to discuss these things.

I get the impression that you hold a lot of guilt and, while it's VERY shitty what you did to that girl, I have full confidence that you have the intellect and sincerity to grow past it if you talk to someone.

Also, early, mid, or late 20s?

VIDEOS THAT ARE WELCOME:
-VIDEOS WITH **REAL** RAPE, BLACKMAIL, FORCED, OR OTHER **RARE** MATERIAL (BLACKMAIL W/ CHATLOG IS BEST)
-BULLY VIDEOS (ONLY W/ NUDITY)
-REAL GROPED GIRLS (NOT ACTED) (EXTREME)
-REAL BUSTED GIRLS DOING NASTY STUFF (LIKE BUSTED SEX WITH ANIMAL OR ANOTHER THING EXTREME)
-REAL UNDERGROUND SEX SLAVE VIDS

►/1404er/ (Mon) 24:10:29
No.3085900600
early 20s.
i better jet. got some things i
need to take care of.

He hit her. He punched her and stamped on her face. He
kicked her where her ribs would have been. The silicon felt
like skin.

►/1404er/ (Mon) 24:12:01
No.3085900605
Ok, but before you go would you
be willing to elaborate on your
relationship with this person
before you did this? Did you
know her well? Know her from
afar? What was your impression
of her?
I mean, beyond her being an idiot
(which is obvious).

After a few days he braved the kitchen again and walked out
with handfuls of knives.

►/1404er/ (Mon) 24:16:01
No.3085900619
look i said had to go. don't look
too deep into this stuff, you won't
find much. it was just some fun at
the time. i did it because i didn't
think it would work, and when it
did i wanted to see how far it
would go. with all these

questions, i get the feeling you'd
do the same.

aight, i'm out.

THANK YOU AND BE SAFE

The doll's limbs and bits trailed through the house. Bloodless and static. He never put his dick in its holes. /1404er/ gathered up the parts and dumped them in the downstairs bathtub and pissed hot toxic orange all over the pieces. Burying them with the dust and ghosts. He screamed and told the pieces they were stupid sluts and deserved all the hell they had coming to them, and did an altogether pretty okay job of keeping himself from crying.

*   *   *

XVII

There was only so much of the world, and he'd seen almost all of it. Even the new and novel began feeling tired and void of sense.

> **▶out with the bathwater**
> **▶/1404er/ (Sat) 16:57:08 No.31004007619**
> Welp, our little one had a small mishap in the bath tonight.
> Figured you guys would appreciate the pics.
> It's cool. She wasn't shaping up to be that much fun anyway.
> ¯_(ツ)_/¯
>
> Download: Bubye.jpg (2.5 mb)

The thumbnail expanded and stretched over the Computer's face. A swollen blue oval atop half-dry porcelain white. Dime-sized eyes froze in odd directions, independent of each other. A thick viscous thread dangled out a black hole mouth, popped open forever. A scrap of paper reading *'sup /1404er/. 2-14-2026.*

> **▶/1404er/ (Sat) 16:59:28 No.31004007632**
> holy shit, op

▶/1404er/ (Sat) 17:01:47 No.31004007639
how old

▶/1404er/ (Sat) 17:07:13 No.31004007656
>>>*31004007639*
not gonna give the exact age, but she was less than a year.
Felt like forever, tho lol

▶/1404er/ (Sat) 17:09:56 No.31004007664
ty for making this the best valentines day ever

▶/1404er/ (Sat) 17:10:50 No.31004007666
shouldve drownd it w yr cock

▶/1404er/ (Sat) 17:13:07 No.31004007674
well done, op. what does its mom think?

▶/1404er/ (Sat) 17:19:33 No.31004007699
>>>*31004007674*
she's cool. We're just sitting tight, drinking some buds, taking it easy.

▶/1404er/ (Sat) 17:20:02 No.31004007700
lul

▶/1404er/ (Sat) 17:41:55 No.31004007738
yr an inspiration to us all
Download: yay.jpg (2 MB)

/1404er/ clicked and another image emerged and swelled. A tiny face on a tangerine head. The tiny face held steady under a faucet head and torrent of furious clear liquid plunged deep down its mouth; down its throat and down its lungs. Puffing

136

cheeks and squeezing eyes migraine-tight. /1404er/'s arms shook. His guts felt like they were about to rot out his orifices.

▶/1404er/ (Sat) 17:44:03 No.31004007750
nice! everyone's killing their babies today

He stared at the walls, but the walls weren't walls anymore. They had changed their composition and characteristics. The walls were infants filled with water, hollow-squishy like balloons. Walls stuffed with them. Walls just piles of flopping infants with eyes at odd angels. An aquarium of squishy infants.

So he watched a movie instead.

They were machines like a human body; a body covered in boxes. And they stretched as tall as to crack the atmosphere. Lots of countries had them, and they were what made the countries disappear. Set out to a pound of war drums, the machines sent tsunamis to drown their homes and foes. World Scalers: Big Dix-3019. When just one was left standing, there wasn't a world to go back to. It only lasted sixty-three minutes.

He woke and it was something ugly fastened to his bathroom's door. Something circular and alien, as if arisen from the ocean's coldest leagues; inhabiting a submerged, slowed motion. Somehow both encumbered and weightless. No face or trace of soul, yet /1404er/ felt it staring right at him.

He'd never seen a house centipede. Awful but made the walls go back to normal. Another appeared.

There was a fist in his chest. /1404er/'s eyes popped wide and teeth ground clenched. The monsters' presence felt like picks through his retina. Sweat carving down his nose. He would swear he heard them talking; that he heard their minuscule voices click and squeak. Unable to make out the words.

►My Wild Ride With A Gov Server
►/1404er/ (Sat) 20:16:47 No.31004009187

TL;DR: I may or may not get v& by the NSA. Fuckit.

Earlier this week,I saw a thread where a guy was on an alleged NSA FTP server. Today, my sense of intrigue got the better of me: I booted up WINGmate, went to an online telnet client, and jumped into the IP the homo had of his 5UP3R 1337 3DG3Y desktop. I logged into a default Micro$oft IIS account for FTP servers (user: ftp), and entered the list command.

Result: Connection closed, IP blocked from server, and likely reported to Homeland Security.

Either way, I've been feeling suicidal and apathetic for months now, so I don't care too much if I get v&. I just find it interesting, I guess. Lulz

►Tarot
►/1404er/ (Sat) 20:14:39
No.31004009178
Let's talk about the Tarot. Mostly
the Major Arcana, but talk about
the Minor is welcome as well.

Another appeared. And a fourth, all emerging from his
bathroom.

He scrambled up out of bed toward the door to the hallway,
jamming his fingers on the knob in his reach to whip it open.
He got through, ran down the hall into the other bathroom and
collapsed in the tub, shrieking. His hands grasped and reached
for anything until one found a bar of half-dissolved soap
(belonging to his father; leftover from death and unused since.
Imbued with the departed's skin cells and curls of thinned
hair). The hand chucked the bar at the mirror above the sink,
and /1404er/ watched the reflective matter spider-web and fall
like shivs.

►/1404er/ (Sat) 20:18:04
No.31004009195
Can anyone give me some
basics of tarot? I mostly use
mirror divination. Also why did
you chose tarot over others
methods of divination?

►/1404er/ (Sat) 20:21:30
No.31004009209
It means whatever you want it to
mean, because fortune telling
doesn't real.

►/1404er/ (Sat) 20:21:33
No.31004009210
considering you were peeping
into a tla box, why the fux did you
think pairing js + telnet together
and logging in directly from your
own device was adequate?

He blew ropes of mucus out his nostrils into shirt fibers and
grabbed heaps of mirror from the floor and sink, letting them
bleed his palms in his rush back to his bedroom. The insects
had doubled in number.

►/1404er/ (Sat) 20:23:08
No.31004009214
why did you not use NDL? are
you retarded?
I am surprised how many people
are not afraid of going inline
without ndl

►/1404er/ (Sat) 20:24:51
No.31004009222
holy fuck lurk moar

►/1404er/ (Sat) 20:27:14
No.31004009235
Get Rider-Waite-Smith, Crowley,
and Marseilles. learn the
difference. You will probably get
a preference, but none are
perfect or indispensable

If you are really trying to tell the
future, you are a dumbass. If

youre using it to meditate on possibilities and realities around you, then you are getting a bit closer to the mark. It is a mirror... you really only see what your mind puts together, but it is an extremely powerful tool for unpacking whats half realized in your brain. If there is any "prediction" it is reading into what your unconscious mind sees as possibilities that your conscious mind wants to ignore.

The walls danced red and white and celestial with each pitch of stained reflective shrapnel, sprayed sharp and tough against the creatures, sending them to the hardwood and onto their backs. Frenzied writhing and almost erotic.

►/1404er/ (Sat) 20:28:00 No.31004009237
maybe they just want to offer you a job

He grabbed fistfuls of action figures, models and bobbleheads from his shelves, smearing the plastic with ripped hands. He threw them at the remaining bodies. Explosions of plastic and carapace, all tumbling to the floor in varying traumas.

►/1404er/ (Sat) 20:29:11 No.31004009240
this is what I suggest you to do now:
0) backup shit you actually need to another drive

1) erase (not delete, erase) your disk. also get rid of any drives or devices that may be interpreted as you are a hacker (like kali linux image cds or USB sticks with hacking tutorials on them)
2) install a fresh system and make it appear like youre a normalfag
3) wait. if nothing happens you might be lucky
4) if the feds show up at your home one day do the following
  a) tell them your computer had viruses a few days ago
  b) you installed a new system with no illegal shit
  c) you feel like you might have been hacked
  d) now it seems ok again
5) with some luck they will trust you and just close the case
6) if not they will take your pc and analyse it.
As you cleansed anything that was on it they should be unable to find anything

▶/1404er/ (Sat) 20:29:02
No.31004009239
I'm so goddamn confused about the meaning of the Moon card. It keeps showing up in readings but nobody seems to give a solid

answer as to what meaning it
has.

He tore the clothes-hanger rod out of his closet and
approached each of the fallen centipedes, blood dribbling
down the rod and the front of his sweatpants. The creature's
legs spasming and grasping for floor and nothing. Bodies
pocked with gaping, bloodless wounds.
/1404er/ choked the rod and stabbed its end down hard on
the squirming creatures, twisting and grinding them into the
wood and dust and pieces of mirror. He raised his spear and
adjusted his aim, and repeated until they all lost qualities
associated with life.

▶/1404er/ (Sat) 20:34:46
No.31004009259
The Moon is the most dangerous
card. If your life is a journey, the
Moon represents the trials you
will face and the tests of your
character, resolve and beliefs
that will confront you along the
way.

▶/1404er/ (Sat) 20:33:05
No.31004009256
This whole plan depends on your
browsing history. If you frequent
skid forums and your ISP logs
gives it to the feds you will be
suspicious to them but here you
might also go with the "this was
not me, some virus must have
done this"-strategy. Therefore in
future use NDL for such stuff.

►/1404er/ (Sat) 20:37:03
No.31004009273
okay so everyone knows the death card isn't necessarily a 'bad omen' or anything, it represents change etc. but in 'understanding thoth tarot' it says 'apparent death or destruction but such interpetation is illusion.' what does that mean? any positive changes usually seem pretty immediately apparent to me

He eased his face into the master bathroom. Two centipedes skittered around the sink's rim; another worked its way up the drain. He stepped back, pulling the door closed tight. He ran back to the hallway bathroom and wrapped his split hands in washcloths. He grabbed eleven towels, fibers all clotted with his father's dust, and returned to his room, stuffing three in the slit beneath the compromised bathroom's door. Then he ran downstairs and pulled out cabinets until he found a roll of duct tape.

►/1404er/ (Sat) 20:44:47
No.31004009310
Again, interpretation of Tarot is just that: interpretation. Nothings set in stone. It's all hugely dependent on the individual doing the reading. Theistics might say that it correlates to the transition from life to afterlife. Or even just the transition from conscious matter and energy to

nonconcious matter and energy. But also psychic death, or the death of something you thought defined you. But it really depends on who you are and how you read the cards

▶/1404er/ (Sat) 20:38:44
No.31004009288
Just say you're sorry. They'll probably let you off with a ~~waterboarding~~ warning.

His hands finally clotted, and the towels taped tight in the cracks around the bathroom door got only slightly crusted with his blood. He wasn't ever going back in. The centipedes had won. It was their bathroom now.

▶/1404er/ (Sat) 20:59:01 No.31004009338
Ok /1404er/ this is OP and this may be my last post cause im SURE im about to get v&. past few nights this van has been parked outside my house from around 10-11pm till early hours. no one gets out no one gets in.

Fast forward to tonight: walking home I see the partyvan parked right outside my front door and some guys taking photos.

I keep walking past my house around block (about 2 miles around est) to kill some time, come back and van is gone. It never goes this early

So yeah fags, this could be my final
goodbye. its been a pleasure and a
nightmare. sayonara

He collapsed in his bed and wept. The insects, when he
pictured them in his head, they looked exactly like him.

*   *   *

►**the observable universe**
►**/1404er/ (Thu) 19:02:17 No.31004531222**
Why is the observable universe a sphere with us at the center? In theory wouldn't that mean light(photons) is coming towards us from all directions?

►**/1404er/ (Thu) 19:07:54 No.31004531249**
Because we can see (roughly) the same distance in every direction. so it defines a sphere centered at where we observe from (here) and yes, that does mean light's coming at us from every direction, but that's nothing particularly dazzling. if you look around you in space there's always going to be stars on all sides of you unless you were at the very edge of the universe for some reason

He scored the batch of unstepped mescaline through Cake Palace, which was pretty much just Blossoms House 6.0. A year since his father passed and his first time with a drug since mom force-fed him antibiotics.

►/1404er/ (Thu) 19:10:06 No.31004531269
But how could it be coming from all directions. The singularity had to be at one point in one direction. That's like a grenade going off in front of you and feeling the shrapnel hitting your back

►/1404er/ (Thu) 19:12:59 No.31004531273
No the singularity was not at one point, it contained everything.

The first half of the trip was like a fever he almost remembered from a decade past, but not unenjoyable. He sank through his mattress and the floor and a beige smear glazed over his eyeballs, and if he concentrated hard enough he could force through the gelatin into the past and change almost anything. He never had a penis. He never stabbed a water bottle with a syringe. He never, ever had the Computer. Within fifteen minutes he had restructured the entirety of his life's arc, and built a person he was okay with living inside. A body and name that hadn't broken the world yet.

►/1404er/ (Thu) 19:14:27 No.31004531287
Yes you are right but once the plasma settled we formed at a point in one direction relative to the original position of the singularity.

►/1404er/ (Thu) 19:15:56 No.31004531290
There is no "relative to the singularity". A singularity isn't even a three-dimensional object, you can't just say it's twenty light years in that direction.

►/1404er/ (Thu) 19:17:00 No.31004531299
In ALL directions. It was chaos, and you
know the thing about chaos? It's fair

He peeled off his clothes, rank and caked with funk, and
walked his house—his parents' house—watching spirals crawl
the walls like circuitry. He knelt at his father's dust, and his
father's love crept below his skin and skull, warm and spiking.
It was a line of warm scarlet drawn from his nostril down past
his lips. His father's heart was with him, even after mother's
apparition had been gone too long to still conjure. He never
knew that when he dreamed, sometimes it was her dream, too.

►/1404er/ (Thu) 19:21:35 No.31004531320
Think of the singularity as the entire
observable universe. As the big bang occurs,
the singularity expands on all sides, shooting
light off in every direction. It's theorized that
the universe may be expanding faster than
the speed of light. If this is true, the
observable universe will always be a sphere
to us, as the things casting that light beyond
that will be too far to see. The actual shape
may be a cone, but we can only see a tiny
bubble inside of said cone.

And regardless that it was a love born of fallacy—the parent's
obligation to love their offspring—he could feel his father's
love persist through him, inside the house; gently dissipating
in its half-life. Making the world take on a vague sort of sense.

►/1404er/ (Thu) 19:25:46 No.31004531345
Is the fact that we are roughly in the middle
of the observable universe "just a
coincidence"? By that I mean: Would it be

possible that in a hypothetical universe with the exact same properties as the one we inhabit now, we could only observe 1 m in some arbitrary direction, making it appear as though we were on the edge of the inside of a sphere?

And then it became five hours sunk and sobbing in the common bathtub, thrashing at his wrists with his father's old, cold-dry shaving razor. Only scraping a top layer of skin cells; scribbling paper cut-caliber abrasions. Throwing a show for himself. A pity party for ghosts.

▶/1404er/ (Thu) 19:31:16 No.31004531401
Because it's what you observe. Every observer has his own Observable Universe as a sphere (since the light is coming from all directions) with him at the center, it just happens that all the known observers are at Earth.

▶/1404er/ (Thu) 19:33:57 No.31004531410
Various Cosmological Horizons.

Despair gave way to malaise. /1404er/ coughed into his scabbed palms and wiped his nose with his elbow. He let the unbloodied razor clatter at the drain. He climbed out of the tub, walked to his room and pulled on his cleanest sullied sweatpants. He shook the dirty-white chunk of plastic with his right hand and woke the Computer up.

▶/1404er/ (Thu) 19:38:04 No.31004531432
Alright, I think I understand why nobody understands my question now. It's probably dumb anyway, but whatever:

As far as my limited understanding of astrophysics goes, the remnant electromagnetic radiation from the big bang is mainly in the microwave part of the spectrum, meaning that e.g. any visible light we can observe must've been emitted by some system of classical particles (e.g. a star).

Is it possible to (theoretically) position yourself in such a way that visible light from systems of classical particles (e.g. stars) is further away from you in an arbitrary direction than it is in another arbitrary direction?

►/1404er/ (Thu) 19:41:59 No.31004531445
Don't know, man. Would be dope as fuck though, I'll give you that

*LivePlateau is the largest aggregator of live webcams found automatically in search engines from all over the world. S*ans-serif lettering printed across the Computer's face. Seventeen-thousand and forty-three cameras. Every aperture a window. Seventeen-thousand and forty-three windows, all stammering arrhythmic. /1404er/ breathed them, one after another. The breaths felt like life become dream; like God alive in the clouds and internal bleeding.

The half-circle of shops and parabolas of Dundee City Square launching out past the frame, strewn aglow with street lamp. The empty flurries and stroked peaks of Big Sky Resort; pick up trucks empty and idle. The dead streets before the city hall in Suensaarenkatu; flash pot warfare at the horizon's wax. The lonesome pole of Buck's Bird Cam. The perforated white and blue light off Westman Islands. Plaza May Albarracín's empty mustard block and blacked out windows. Ukkohalla Ski & Sport Resort's greyscale, all swollen with ghosts. Fossen School's grounds, all brown-toxic and wet.

Some of it was ten years of plague; no people but their traces. Some places had always been that way at night. But the world goes on forever. The world goes on and on. No matter the method which time is dictated, the world goes on and on.

Smog cloaks Nagasaki Port at their noon. Cars stutter in serpentine along the Atami-kaigan Expressway. The Sōjijiso-in Temple is wind blowing leaves and banners glancing off clay-shingled roofs. The Takimidai Waterfall bisects orange and green below fog, carving down past the frame. And still, the SIK Hockey arena in Storuman, Sweden is just red circles and targets and blue letters over beige under shadow. The Drachten Animal Hospital Dog Room rotted floor and chair and no life. United Print is over a hundred Germans binding books.

A figure stands at the end of a Staten Island driveway with a knife in its hand. Maybe only men are left.

And still, /1404er/ sees the clouds bisect the atmosphere bottom to top, setting creases of a halo upon ocean's skin. He sees above the rooftops and wires of Isapa Home Area toward choked skies; teardrop blues and crusted pinks congealed under white. Mashike Harbour sky is the color of cartilage. The color of spoiled harvest.

The greens of endless dark far past beyond the rocks and ripples—looking out over Cape Nosappu. Vast as the ordered tilt of Seia Portugal. The Póstelek Park division of trees and light across concrete; coppering like rot.

The mountains across Kiyosato, a knife scraped and swept back. Durango a photo from after the bombs dropped.

And still, Szombathely Square is human and coital with writhings ghosted to glass. Metro Club is eleven Ukrainians line dancing to North American pop. Corso Del Popolo alive as a Viking wake. IAC Observatory a faux-biblical heaven;

clouds below and figures circling stairs like pre-suicide. Straw grass and white bark burning brown old Edmonton; shriveled to aging human forms.

Nantucket Harbor sinking under its grey. Blotted with deformed mammoth flies. Miyoshi an Earth-swallowing fissure. Bristol Head Acres a place to die secluded and comfortable.

No one realizes they walk the same as others. No one makes war at the Kamba Waterfall Monkey Park. The Hiroshima Peace Memorial is buffered in outstretched green. Hyoban-do is all behavior and routine, ascribed faces, bodies and names. Intuition. Skin and insides wet warm like a birth or a car crash. Butterflies snapping frame to frame before Yuki Jinja Shrine.

/1404er/ didn't measure the hours, or days, or condition of his body. He didn't feel his hunger or fatigue. He was somewhere else now. Someplace separate from his walls, or room, or house, or the Computer and its history. He lay his palms flat on the desk, and stared into endless blue—the skies above Hirasawa Pass, 9:04 PM his time. Beyond the blue an impenetrably cold vastness, dotted with untrod terrains and points of hot nuclear light. A space with no thought or breath; no malevolence or consideration. A space perfect and vacuous, encasing him in his world and all that had ever belonged to it.

END

SCHiSM²

Made in the USA
Columbia, SC
16 August 2022

65470143R00121